The Obituary Girl

A novel

Paul Paré

The Obituary Girl

ISBN – E-book: 978-1-963539-08-0

ISBN - Paperback: 978-1-963539-18-9

First Edition: March 2024

Disclaimer

This novella is a work of fiction. Unless stated otherwise, all the names, businesses, places, characters, events, and incidents are either a product of the author's imagination or used in a fictitious manner. Any resemblance to actual persons, living or dead, or events is purely coincidental. The author does not endorse, condone, or promote any actions or ideologies depicted in this novella. Reader discretion is advised.

Table of Contents

ONE

THE WOMAN WHO SPEAKS TO BIRDS

She takes the granite steps one at a time, deliberately, planting her feet firmly on one step before tackling the next. She counts out loud as she climbs: "Three, four, five," a heavy gasp punctuating each movement. A cluster of fallen leaves retreats before the hem of her bathrobe as she climbs. "Eight," she says with a tone of final authority.

Anne Marie leans against the heavy door and pats her breast in a routine gesture intended to calm her racing heart. She reaches for the brass handle and swiftly withdraws her hand. "Ah! That could be cold." Pulling at her sleeve to form a mitten, she grasps the handle. It doesn't budge. She tries again. "What? Is it locked?" She gives it one more tug. "It cannot be locked," she cries out. "They never lock the church! Not during the day. At night, of course, they lock it. But at this time of day, never. People come and go and these doors are always kept unlocked."

Bewildered, she looks around her, turning and stretching slowly, peering in all directions, making sure she's at the right place. The brickwork with its niches and statues is familiar. So is the steeple rising above her to greet the November sun. "This *is Notre-Dame* Church,

Notre-Dame de la Consolation?" She pulls herself forward just enoug to see the lintel above the door. She reads the gothic letters and murmur *N-D de la Consolation – 1902*. "Yes, of course. I know this place; I hav been here hundreds of times." She tries the handle again, shaking it a much as her frail body allows. To make noise. To let someone know she' at the door. Nothing happens. "Jesus! Jesus!" she cries out. And the quickly she regrets: "Oh no! No, Jesus, I am not angry, I am not usin your name in vain. I am simply asking you to help."

Anne Marie's eyes tighten as she scans the brick terrac surrounding the façade, searching and finding the large cement benc facing the archway. She climbs down and walks to the bench an collapses onto it. She holds her hands before her mouth watching he breath steam against the coolness of the air. Her determination to reac the church was banishing all fear and pushing her beyond reality Suddenly she knows it, confronting the knowledge and accepting it in th same way she's learned to face the humiliations of the past few months.

"I am an 82-year-old woman and, of course, I am going to do sill things." Slowly, she pulls the blanket around her shoulders and squeeze it against her legs as the wind picks up a batch of dead leaves and send them coasting in front of her.

Anne Marie finds the metal sign attached to the back of the bench "In Memoriam." She examines the names and dates appearing beneath i She stops at the most recent: "*Le Révérend Père Roger Laroche - 1972.* She reads it to herself several times, her smile swelling. She reviews i her mind the moment when she was first introduced to Father Laroche "That was so long ago, but I will never forget you," she whispers as sh caresses the name on the plaque. Her thoughts are interrupted by the nois rush hour traffic and the sound of a far-off siren from a police car, a fir truck, or perhaps an ambulance. "You know, Father. Those were som truly inspiring days, and you played such an important role in my life, Anne Marie says in an intimate tone while taking a couple of dee breaths.

She continues, "Oh, but in recent years…How my life has changed I was better off left alone." She pauses and silently counts her breaths

"Why, why did they take me to that home? Oh, it is very grand; I have my own little room and I do not have to worry about anything."

"But, I miss my canaries – all three of them." Amusement fills her eyes. "I named them after the Trinity: Father, Son, and Holy Ghost. The white one was The Holy Ghost." Mischief infects her voice. Anne Marie looks up behind her to the church door. "Jesus, oh, you will forgive me for that, won't you? You understand the authorities refused to let me bring them with me to the Home. Oh, I do hope someone has adopted them. I hope they have been kept together. They got along so well and caused no trouble."

"Those ladies I live with have cold hearts. They are cruel. They are not aware of the comfort given to me by those lovely birds." Her smile contorts into a scowl. She takes a deep breath and coughs. "Everybody says I talk too much, and to myself most of the time. These ladies at that home, they do not know me, they have no idea who I am." Anne Marie brings her hands to her mouth and exhales a warming mist. "I was a pioneer; I had a career, I was well-known, I was so successful! Ah, the first female member of the newsroom at The Great Falls Evening Tribune. I had more than my share of bylines: A. M. Dubois, often on Page One. Everyone knew me, everyone read me. I was quoted by other media...often!"

She pauses, she glances upwards at the cross atop the steeple. "You know, Jesus, I cannot be expected to live forever. I am weak and tired all the time. I hope you do not mind if I come here and talk to you. I know we were not particularly close in recent years, but I have come back to you." She stands up and with new-found strength and determination, reclimbs the steps to the church door and places her ear against the wooden panel. "Please. Please. There is a penitent here, one seeking final absolution, one who must cleanse her soul before meeting her creator." Anger shrouds her voice. "This is not a social call. Open the door!" Slowly, she turns and faces the street in her flowing robe. Her blanket falls off her shoulder as she yells out to the wind and the traffic: "I have also led a sinful life. Fame and notoriety can lead to depravity. *Le bon Père Laroche* became aware of some of this."

Anne Marie faces the street and continues her harangue. "It was many, many years ago. But now, I am here. I am here today at my lifetime parish. I am here to seek forgiveness and acceptance into your holy kingdom." She uses the words and the tone she remembers from the mouths of preachers and homilists. Anne Marie crumbles back against the door. "*Mon Dieu, ah, mon Dieu.*"

Slowly she manages to control her breathing. Her voice is weak. "Those women I live with, they are the crazy ones. They are jealous because I am among the oldest and yet I am the prettiest. They despise that," she whispers. "I *have* retained my youthful glow. This is not vanity, nothing to confess here. I was always pretty – not beautiful, but pretty." She smiles at the word 'pretty.' Her smile fades. "However, that is what led to depravity, this is what got me into trouble. That was the root of my sin."

Anne Marie returns to the bench; she buries her head and stares at the dead leaves gathering around her like an old tree trunk. Once again, she hears sirens as they wail feebly in the distance. She hates the sound of sirens. "The men in the newsroom loved to hear them. It meant a story. I hated that sound. It meant bad news."

The early evening shadows intrude into the space. Even if some passing motorists bother to look at the old church, no one would see Anne Marie stooped in the shadows. "Oh, Jesus. Oh, my sweet Jesus, I need to find you and to confess, to openly repent." She starts to cry again. Her sobs are cavernous. Withdrawing even deeper into the bench, she leans down and brushes away the fallen leaves that cling to the corners of her refuge.

She hears his voice.

"Miss Dubois. There you are."

"Jesus! – Jesus? You are here after all."

"No. Miss Dubois. It's Tom. Huh, I've been called many things, but never Jesus. I've come to take you home. Here, come with me now. Be a good girl."

"I am not a good girl, as you put it."

Tom ignores her remarks as he pulls her up gently out of her seat at the church entry. Despite her aching shoulder and a weak right knee, she gives no resistance and follows him to the waiting van, squinting at the vehicle, reading out loud the blue lettering on its side: "Laura F. Washburn Home." She repeats the name and sighs.

"I'm so glad we found you. It's getting too cold for these escapades."

"Do not worry, Tom. They know me here. This is my church, I am safe here," she replies.

Tom cautiously walks her to the street and escorts her to the passenger side of his van. "No, thank you, young man." Tom gives her a surprised look. Silence follows as the two face each other. Suddenly, Anne Marie reaches for the back door. "Roomier back here." Tom reaches for the door, opens it wide, and assists his passenger as she fits herself into the rear of the vehicle.

"You remind me so much of the college kids who would spend a few months at the newspaper each summer. Interns, we called them. They were so eager and motivated and wanting to please," she says from the back seat.

"I suppose that's a compliment."

"It can be. And your reddish hair reminds me of one of those students. It was 1988, the year I retired from the paper. He was a journalism major at the University of Massachusetts, and he had the brightest red hair and pink pimples on the white skin of his neck and forehead. He was very smart, but none of the regulars in the newsroom took him seriously. I, however, admired his dedication. And, oh yes, one day he showed up for work wearing a bright green shirt and someone tagged him the strawberry-rhubarb kid, and everybody laughed, so the name stuck for the remainder of the summer. I felt sorry for him. He was such a sweet boy."

Tom doesn't pay attention to his passenger's ramblings as he pulls away from the parking space. "All right, let's get you back to the nursing home safely." He locks the rear door with a loud latching mechanism that reinforces in Anne Marie's mind that she's really a prisoner at the Washburn Nursing Home. At a stop sign, Tom hands her a folded copy of the day's newspaper. "Today's paper. I know how you like to read it."

Anne Marie releases the blanket from her shoulders and places the newspaper on the seat next to her. She reads the date under the masthead: "Tuesday, November 6, 2008." Realizing the paper is one day old, she wants to tell Tom that it's yesterday's edition, but decides not to. "Thank you, Tom. I appreciate that. You know, I worked at The Tribune. I was the first woman reporter. But you know that, don't you? Everybody at the Washburn Home is aware of my newspaper career, although no one seems to care, or at least none of my fellow suffragettes want to talk about it."

"Suffrawhats? Who is that? Does that mean someone who suffers? Is that a French word?"

"Not really. But it sounds like a French word: a woman who suffers. But the real suffragettes were pioneer women. Women who fought for the right to vote – just like men had the right to vote. And they finally won after many years of protesting. You have never heard that expression, Tom? Everybody called them suffragettes. That is how I refer to the other residents of the home. I mean it as a joke of course. Few of the ladies have ever caught on, though."

"Were you a suffragette, Miss Dubois?"

"Of course not, young man. Your education is sadly lacking, oh my! Those women won the right to vote long before I was born. But at the newspaper office, we had our own battles."

"Well, Miss Dubois, sometime you can tell me all about your newspaper battles."

The van slows and turns into the driveway of the nursing home. Anne Marie doesn't pay attention. Her eyes closed, she replays her first lays at the newspaper, how she balanced fear and enthusiasm, how she ried to absorb everything all at once.

"Here we are, home sweet home. Take my hand, and lean on my houlder. Be careful, Miss Dubois. I'll walk slowly."

"Do not talk to me like I am an old cripple, Tom. I can take care of nyself."

"Just doing my job. Just doing my job."

"Listen to you, repeating things all the time. You sound just like us, he old suffragettes inside the nursing home. Hee, hee, hee!"

The two slowly climb the set of steps leading to the front entrance. As Tom opens the oak door, Anne Marie pulls the sleeve of her robe over her hand and gently sweeps the etched glass of the central window. "You now, Tom, this was one of the grandest houses in Great Falls. Impressive /ictorian. Fine detail. Modestly decorated though, all in such good taste."

"I'm sure it was," Tom says, as he escorts her through the reception rea where they are greeted by Betsy, the afternoon receptionist.

"Oh, so they found you. What an example you set, trotting off like hat, going wherever you please, whenever you please. Who do you think 'ou are, anyway?"

"Betsy, Betsy, Betsy. Calm down, will you?" Anne Marie replies.

Anne Marie takes Tom's arm and the two walk down the main corridor. "Now, where was I? Oh, yes, I was telling you about this house. t belonged to the Central Maine Literary Society, you know. Before that, his was the residence of Laura F. Washburn, a famous writer of the late 800s. After she died, the house became the headquarters of the literary ociety. Miss Washburn left it to them in her will, you understand. They had poetry readings, they had tea every Friday afternoon and, of course, hey maintained an extensive library – books written by women, only vomen: novels, memoirs, poetry, travel books, books for children. The nembers, however, did not care much for the idea of women writing for newspapers. That was not literary, they believed."

"That's interesting, Miss Dubois. Here's your room," Tom says.

Inside, Anne Marie keeps on. "Once they held a reception for U.S
Senator Margaret Chase Smith. You have heard of her haven't you, Tom
The ladies thought that a woman newspaper reporter would be a fin
addition to the audience, and they invited me. But I was warned that thi
was a social event, not a press conference, and I would not be allowed t
throw questions at their guest of honor. *Throw* is the word they used an
when the time came, I was introduced to Senator Smith as a local reporte
They did not even mention my name, would you believe it? I think thos
fancy ladies were as afraid of my French name as much as my choice c
work. Senator Smith did pull me aside at one point and we talked briefl
about newsgathering. She was very, very pleasant, unlike her hostesses.
Anne Marie takes a deep breath. "Now, those uppity ladies are gone, thei
library is empty, the contents donated to the Maine State Library i
Augusta. The grand society is defunct, this grand old building is a nursin
home, a place where a gaggle of old women wait for their turn to b
defunct."

"I'm impressed. You seem to know so much about this house. Now
make yourself comfortable and I'll tell Mrs. Wiggins you've returnec
She's very worried about you. She told me you skipped your afternoo
medications."

Anne Marie ignores the comment. She's deep into the notion tha
those fancy ladies would be so upset that a newspaper reporter is livin
at the Central Maine Literary Society. "My, my, they would turn over i
their graves." She takes a series of breaths that turn into crafty snicker
"Oh, my, just listen to me talk on and on. Just like *une vielle pie*. Yo
know, that is what we as children would call our aunt Germaine. It is
French expression that refers to a magpie, a bird that keeps on twitterin
all the time," she says to Tom who smiles and gently closes the doc
behind him.

Alone, she turns on the lamps and starts to fold her blanket. Sh
goes to hang it in her closet and, as she pulls the drape, she sees the frame
photos of her canaries. "Ah, my little ones. At least I still have the picture
of you three. How are you doing? I certainly hope that someone has foun

a way to cherish you as much as I have. Just look at you! You are so handsome, with your fine little plumage. And your eyes still shine. Oh my, oh my…"

Mrs. Wiggins, the nursing supervisor, tiptoes into the room and is surprised to find it empty. She throws a worried look at the small space and wonders if her patient has gone on another escapade. Suddenly, she hears a human voice chirping away. She pulls back the drape and smiles. "Good evening, Miss Dubois. There you are." Anne Marie walks out of her enclosure and stands facing Mrs. Wiggins, a short woman in her late sixties who uses her manner of speech to prop herself up.

"I'm here with your pills; I have a full month's dosage of each prescription," she says in a commanding voice.

"Just leave them on the dresser, Mrs. Wiggins. I will take them later."

"I'm afraid we can't do that. I have to make sure you take them. I have to watch you. You know that. Now, there are three pills. I'll give them to you one by one and you can take a sip of water after each one. Do you want to sit by the bedside?"

Anne Marie follows her into a corner of the room, sits on the edge of her bed.

"So, here, let's take your pills. Number one, in your mouth, now a gulp of water, open wide, let me see if you've swallowed it. Ok. Now, pill number two, water, swallow, let me see…"

"Please, please do not treat me like a baby," Anne Marie utters.

"I'm sorry, but these are the procedures. Some time ago, one of our residents passed and in a drawer in her dresser we found over two years' worth of pills. Not one of them taken during all that time."

"Well, obviously, she did not need them," Anne Marie says with a tone of vindication.

"What's obvious is that she did need them, and had she taken them as prescribed, she would have lived longer."

"Maybe she stopped taking them because she didn't want to live any longer. Did anyone think of that?"

"Miss Dubois, don't be so contrarian. Here we go with pill number three."

Mrs. Wiggins gives in to her irritation. "And, I have to say that you have been warned often about leaving the Washburn Home by yourself. You simply cannot walk off like that anytime you feel like it. We would be held responsible if anything happened to you."

"I just went outside for a while. Felt the need to get some fresh air, to get some exercise."

"Well, Miss Dubois, you know we offer exercise classes every other day, specifically designed for someone your age."

"You mean those women from the Great Falls Agility Academy? Goodness, talk about the blind leading the blind…"

"Enough with your sarcasm. It's very annoying, you should know. Now, I have other residents to care for. I will put these pill bottles in the top drawer of your dresser. The rules say that's where they should be kept, and that's where we – myself or someone else from the staff will find them and help you with them every afternoon. Now, you can return to your little closet for some quiet time with, with, eh, your birds, if you wish."

Less than fifteen minutes later, Mrs. Wiggins returns and vents a barrage of complaints. "Miss Dubois, Tom just told me that he found you at the old Catholic Church on Pine Street. He says that's not the first time. You must have walked there. Did you walk there? Of course, you did. In the cold and the wind, and in the near darkness. What are you thinking, Miss Dubois?" Her voice is jarring as she holds back the drape that moments before had shielded Anne Marie. "You know we are responsible for you, legally and otherwise."

Anne Marie winces as she rises from her alcove. "I am not a prisoner here. I must do what I must do. I must go where I must. You cannot stop me."

"But there are procedures. Rules to follow. You can't just come and go as you please. We are responsible for your safety. You know that. You read all the forms that you signed when you came to reside with us. You understood it then." She pauses. "For the care and safety provided by Laura F. Washburn Home, you gave up some freedoms, like coming and going as you please. You signed the papers."

Anne Marie drops herself onto the lounge chair. She remains quiet for several moments and then offers in a low voice. "But, Mrs. Wiggins, I must go to church."

"I see. Yes, Tom told me. And I can understand that. But I just checked your admission papers and there's nothing about a religious affiliation on your part. If there were, we would have to respect that. And we are open to all denominations; we have clergymen of all sorts come here for our residents."

"There is only one church for me: *Notre-Dame de la Consolation*, where I was this afternoon. That is the church of my childhood. That is where I must return."

"They closed that church several months ago. There's no one there. I'm sorry, but that is what it is. They put up some 'No Trespassing' signs. Didn't you see them?"

"No Trespassing. No. They cannot do that. I did not see those signs; if I had, I would have torn them down myself."

"Well, I'm sure they're still there. You didn't see them! I guess some people don't see what they don't want to see," the nursing home supervisor offers with satisfaction.

Anne Marie reacts to the silence that follows. She looks about searching for a place to hide – an escape route. She feels the dryness of the forced heat in the small room, she is surprised by the tears that cluster in her eyes and the breaths that ache through the weakness of her shoulders and her arms. "No. No, no." She keeps the words to herself. "No. No." Again, to herself, a weapon to help her maintain control. She struggles to calm her breathing; she flutters her eyelids to stop the welling. Finally, she mutters in a slow, deliberate voice, "I will not allow myself to let you know, Mrs. Wiggins, how desperate you have made me feel."

Mrs. Wiggins finds a subdued tone. "Listen, Miss Dubois, we'll try to come to some accommodation. Let me see what I can do." Her eyes wander about the room, seeing nothing unusual. She checks her large golden watch hanging from a ribbon loop around her neck. "The supper bell should be ringing soon, and I expect to see you for supper. You understand me, dearie?"

Anne Marie shrugs in acceptance. She watches Mrs. Wiggins walk out of the room. Anne Marie returns to her closet and draws the drape tightly behind her. Making herself comfortable on the small vanity seat she had Tom rescue from a pile of discarded furniture, she peruses her little haven: clothing pushed to one end, leaving a free wall above a small bureau covered by framed first pages of the Tribune with her bylined articles, and next to them some binders with letters to the editor praising her work, a few folders containing some of her research, a pair of matted black and white photographs of Anne Marie and her mother, and finally the colored photos of her canaries. She caresses the pictures of the birds one by one. Her eyes closed tightly, she whispers "Father, Son, and Holy Ghost."

TWO

THE OBITUARY GIRL

Ed Lesnick looked up from his desk and spotted the young woman standing in the doorway of the newsroom. "Yes, Miss… Eh, can I help you?"

The newcomer didn't hear him. She was overwhelmed by the sound of typewriters, the ring of telephones, the voices of men sitting at desks packed into a small space. Attached to the ceiling, an ever-rolling metal bar sent annoying clicks through the room as it carried pieces of paper in and out of the area. The young girl noticed the man at the corner desk place some copy paper in a clasp and attach it to the metal bar. The man moved towards her, half-smiling. "My name is Ed Lesnick; I'm the editor. Can I help you?"

She took a few steps forward. "My name is Anne Marie Dubois and the receptionist in the hallway sent me in here." She spoke in a low voice. "I'm interested in the job listed on the job bank radio program."

Ed placed his hand on her shoulder and gently nudged her out of the newspaper office and onto the sidewalk in front of the Tribune office. "First thing, young lady, if you want to work here, you'll have to speak up. Loud and clear. Gets terribly noisy in there." He smiled at her an saw in her his own daughter when she had gone job hunting. "So Miss…eh, Miss…"

The girl volunteered: "Dubois."

"Yes. Dubois. You pronounce it Doobway, as in French."

"Well, it is French, and it really should be said Dubou-ah – Dubou ah."

"I see, that may take getting used to."

"My father would have disowned me if he had ever heard me sa Duboys," she replied, adding "but we can avoid the problem: just call m Anne Marie." She smiled at him.

Ed was slightly put off by her bravado. He adopted a stern voic and looked at his wristwatch. "So, you want to work at a newspaper. D you have any idea what you might want to do here?"

"In the newsroom, of course. A reporter. That's what the job ban said was available."

"And you know what a reporter does?"

"Well, I've been reading the newspaper since I was in the fift grade. Every day, practically. And I've seen every movie abou newspapers and reporters."

"I see…How are your typing skills? Do you have a car? Or, at leas a driver's license?"

"My typing skills are quite good. My family can't afford a car. W take the bus. And, since we don't have a car, I don't have a license." Ann Marie suddenly envisioned herself as handicapped: how can I cover th news if I can't get to where things are happening?

The editor stated that the newspaper had a fleet of cars available i the back lot. He browsed through his memory to determine if any femal ever drove one of them and concluded that none had. "If we get to that point, I'm sure we can get you some driving lessons."

Standing in the doorway, the editor and the aspiring journalist shuffled more than once as individuals entered or left the building. Anne Marie had a perfect view of the Public Library across the street, the massive brick City Hall on the opposite corner, and almost next door the grand old Whitney Hotel where everyone of importance stayed. She knew the area well and dreamed of becoming a part of the bustle and rush of downtown.

"Did you go to college, Miss Dubois?"

"Yes, Bliss College here in town. I wanted to go to Bates or Bowdoin, but we couldn't afford it. I have an associate degree in business management and for the past two years I've worked as the assistant bookkeeper at Graham's Department Store."

"So, you're good with numbers…"

"Yes, but that's not what I want to do with my life. I need adventure, I need to be in the midst of things, part of connecting the public with what's happening. Yes, I can handle figures and ledgers, but my passion lies with words – sentences that resonate and have long-lasting meaning." She stopped, realizing she sounded too eager and too ambitious. "And I would hope for the opportunity to use my enthusiasm on behalf of the readers of The Great Falls Evening Tribune, ah…with the right mentoring of course."

She waited for the editor to respond. Both Anne Marie and the editor looked up at the recent headlines hand-written on newsprint pages hanging from wires in the front windows. Again, Ed checked his watch. "Well, Anne Marie, you evidently know what you want, and you can express it forcibly. Actually, you sound like you're running for office." He laughed and told her to see the receptionist and fill out a job application before leaving. "Young lady, I'll get back to you as soon as I can."

"You did what?" Anne Marie's mother growled at her. "Did I hear you right? You went to the newspaper office looking for a job. Is that what you just told me?" Standing in the kitchen, the older woman never looked away from the stove where she was preparing supper. She simply yelled at her daughter, throwing her words here and there in the cramped space, confident they would strike their destination. "I just can't believe it," she went on. "You already have a job. What's wrong with the one you've got? You should be proud to work in the office at the city's largest department store. Much, much better than working at the shoe shop. Goodness' sake, it took me ten years to make my way up to fancy stitcher. And all I got was a measly twelve-cent raise. And I still get laid off twice a year when it slows down at the shop. You've been at Graham's Department Store just under two years and you're the assistant bookkeeper and everybody knows Miss Riley is going to retire soon and you'll be first in line for the job. No layoffs, no dirt, no noise. It's a good job, Anne Marie, with a good future. You want to give all that up? Besides, what in God's name would you do at a newspaper office anyways? Those are all men's jobs."

Anne Marie said nothing. Finally, she walked out onto the side porch of their fourth-floor apartment. She felt dizzy. Going to the newspaper office had exhausted her. She didn't need to be grilled by her mother. She sat on the glider and blocked out the screams of the Callahan kids below. She stared at the neighboring tenement building a few feet away with its array of side porches where Mrs. Laliberté was stretching to hang the day's wash. "Is that my future? Hanging laundry and cooking meals in a tenement on Blake Street, with kids screaming all day?"

"Anne Marie? Anne Marie, can you hear me?"

"Yes, *Maman*."

"Go get your brother. He should be in the park playing basketball. Supper's going to be ready in ten minutes."

For three days, Anne Marie kept expecting some word from Mister Lesnick, but there was none. She listened to the job bank radio report, to hear if the job notices would still include the position in the newsroom. Each time her hopes plummeted. "The Great Falls Evening Tribune is looking to add to its newsgathering staff. Applicants should have a thorough knowledge of the area, fast typing skills, and be able to provide a writing sample."

Anne Marie was certain that the original notice didn't include a writing sample. She hadn't submitted one nor had Mister Lesnick asked for one. She didn't know what to make of this. Were they fine-tuning the pool of applicants? Was this a way to avoid inexperienced job seekers? She was confident in her writing skills but had no way of showing it. Should she make something up, maybe a phony story about a fire at Graham's Department Store? Anne Marie had read countless accounts of fires, and she became enslaved to the idea, spending time at her desk writing in long hand a variety of scenarios.

Miss Riley, the bookkeeper, noticed how distracted her assistant was but said nothing.

After work on the fourth day, Anne Marie went to the public library and asked to use a typewriter. She transcribed her notes about the make-believe fire and smiled as she headed home, pledging to take the sample to Mister Lesnick during her lunch break the next day.

"You're late for supper. Did you have to work late? Where were you? In any event, there's nothing left. Your brother ate everything. André asked me if he could have it. He's a growing boy, you know, getting stronger all the time." *Maman* Dubois was drying the dishes as she aimed her bombardment of questions at Anne Marie. She wiped the kitchen counter clean and waved her daughter out of her way. "You might as well go out on the porch and sit on the glider like you do every night. There's nothing left for you to eat."

Anne Marie stood silently, then grabbed the copy of the day's newspaper before leaving the kitchen. It was too dark to read on the porch, so she went into her tiny bedroom. The paper would be her supper, she thought. She knew her mother really didn't expect a response from her. It had nothing to do with being late for supper. *Maman* was agitated because, once again, she was bracing herself for the usual October layoff at the shoe shop. This, Anne Marie knew too well. The layoff and lack of pay would rule the household for the next several weeks. As she closed her bedroom door, she mumbled to herself, "You need to get that job, young lady."

At exactly 12 noon the next day, Anne Marie left the store and walked to the newspaper office. Standing in the reception area, she was surprised by the commotion stemming from the newsroom. She nudged her way into the room only to be overwhelmed by shouts and cheers. The room was packed with reporters, secretaries, receptionists, matronly ladies who might be from the Social Desk, photographers, older men in suits and ties, a cluster of workers who looked like they were from the print shop with their heavy aprons and paper hats. Everyone was standing, all looking towards an alcove where a self-important-looking little man was reading in a loud voice the words trickling from the wire service printers. Anne Marie caught a few words: Eisenhower, Italy, evacuations. She heard hurrahs and applause. She spotted Mister Lesnick in the middle of the crowd.

"Well, that's official: General Eisenhower has just announced that Italy has surrendered to the Allies," the little man said to the assembly.

Ed Lesnick caught sight of Anne Marie, smiled, and waved to her. She was stunned not only by the announcement and the commotion it generated but also by the editor's smile. He made his way toward her, pushing through the crowd. "Miss Dubois, I'm glad you stopped by. Hope you don't mind all this brouhaha, but you understand this is a very important development in the war. I'd like to introduce you to the publisher. He's the one who read the wire and who made the announcement. It's quite significant for him since his grandmother was from Italy." They tried to make their way to the publisher, but the crowd pushed them away. Finally, Mister Lesnick took Miss Dubois by the arm and escorted her into the hallway. "I was going to call you. The job is yours. Can you start next Monday? Be here at 8 a.m."

"Oh..." She hesitated. "Of course, but...but the radio nnouncement still included the newsgathering job. I thought you were till looking...and that you were still interviewing applicants..."

"Haven't had time to change the radio ad, sorry about that. Don't vorry, the job is yours," the editor said.

"Mister Lesnick, I don't know what to say. Thank you. Thank you o much. Of course, I'll be here, bright and early."

"And what's that in your hand? Something for me to read?"

She hesitated. "No, it's nothing. Some notes, that's all."

"Ok. See you Monday," he said as he returned to the newsroom.

Anne Marie couldn't help thinking this was the life she would ecome a part of. She folded her writing sample and said in a low voice, 'Not now, a fake fire at Graham's can't compare to the fall of Italy." By he time she reached the sidewalk, she was laughing furiously.

Walking back to the department store, Anne Marie wondered how he would tell Miss Riley about the new job. "There's no doubt I have to; Monday's just a few days away. But, how do I say it, what words do I se?"

Miss Riley had been her only boss. She had taken Anne Marie in traight out of business school, had introduced her to the particulars of an ffice in a very large and very busy department store, and had been patient nd nurturing. Of late, she had made it clear that when she retires, the osition of head bookkeeper would be Anne Marie's. It was how things an at Graham's. Each department head had a say about his or her uccessor, except the men's department where poor old Mister Coolidge ad no say because his job went to one of the Graham sons. That was well efore Anne Marie, but it was common knowledge, and all the old-timers vere more than willing to let everyone know the decision had been a isaster.

Anne Marie was rehearsing her announcement as she stood by th
elevator. The elevator attendant opened the door and the two smiled
each other.

"How was your lunch break, Miss Dubois?"

"Please John. Don't call me that. It makes me feel old. You know
you and I are the same age and we've gone to the movies together a fe
times. So, call me Anne Marie. Please."

"Anne Marie is the pretty girl I took to the Strand; Miss Dubois
the assistant bookkeeper where I work. Miss Dubois works in the upstai
office. I'm the elevator boy. I open and close the door for Miss Dubois.

"But you wear a uniform, and it makes you look so handsome."

"Fourth floor. Here we are. Have a nice afternoon, Miss Dubois.
John grinned and winked at her as she stepped out of the elevator.

Anne Marie returned the smile along with her "Thank you." For
moment, she wondered if she would find someone to flirt with at th
newspaper office.

Miss Riley took a rigid approach to the announcement, sittin
stiffly at her large mahogany desk, her hands folded, not looking directl
at her assistant. "This is your decision, yours alone, not influenced b
anything or anyone here at Graham's?"

"Of course. Miss Riley, I want you to know that I will forever b
grateful for the opportunity you have given me here. I have learned s
much…"

"So, your mind is made up. This is final." Miss Riley starte
browsing through the day's mail stacked in the IN box. She looked
Anne Marie with a questioning and slightly hopeful look. "You're sur
about this?"

"Yes, ma'am."

"And when do you start at the newspaper?"

Anne Marie cleared her throat and cast her gaze at the oversized calendar on the wall. "Well, I've been told to show up Monday morning, bright and early."

"Next Monday?"

"Yes, next Monday."

"Goodness, today's Thursday and the day is nearly over. That gives you tomorrow to wrap things up here. Not much notice, young lady." She spoke in a formal tone.

"I'm so sorry about that. I have no choice. They need me there first thing Monday."

"They NEED you?" she yelled out. "Are you sure you're not exaggerating? Listen, Anne Marie, this is far from satisfactory. You may have to work Saturday, just to make sure you leave everything in good order." The bookkeeper turned her attention to the ledgers occupying a corner of her desk.

"Of course, Miss Riley. I'll do everything I can to make for an easy transition."

"And, of course, you may have to work here evenings for a few days if that becomes necessary. Oh! My God! This is such short notice. I know what they're going to do. You know how they're going to handle this, don't you? They're going to send old Mrs. Graham to take your place. You know, the owner's mother, she used to be the bookkeeper here...hundreds of years ago. Oh! My God!"

"Again, Miss Riley, I'm so sorry."

"Well, I hope they're paying you enough at the newspaper. I hope it's going to be worth it for you to leave me in such a ruckus. How much are they paying you, Anne Marie?"

The hesitation in the office was overwhelming.

"Miss Riley. I really don't know. I didn't think to ask."

Monday morning couldn't come too soon, but when the alarm rang at 6 o'clock, the insistent tone startled Anne Marie into the reality of her new job. Doubts forced her to lie in bed for a few extra minutes. "You did what?" she said, borrowing her mother's words. "You did what?" she repeated until the tin alarm clock overspent its ringing mechanism.

"You did what? You did what?" she mumbled all the way down the hall to the bathroom. She faced the mirror and questioned her reflection. "Who do you see there, Anne Marie Dubois? Do you see a daring young woman about to embark on a new venture? Or do you see the face of delusion? Which is it, Anne Marie Dubois? True adventure or wasteful desire?"

"Anne, let me use the bathroom. I gotta pee." She heard her brother's whining.

"Well, I'll have to wait and see what the day brings," Anne Marie whispered to the early-morning visage in the mirror. She grabbed her pouch of toiletries and opened the door. "It's all yours, little brother."

She rushed back to her tiny bedroom and reviewed the array of clothing she had spread out on a chair the night before, examining each item carefully for its correctness. "What kind of impression do you want to create on your first day?" She discarded the maroon blazer, deeming it too mannish a statement, replacing it at first with a black sweater and then with a gray one. She felt the gray sweater was a better match with her plaid skirt. "Demure is the impression I want to convey," she said out loud. "Yes, demure! Just the right touch of professionalism tinged with modesty." She paraded in front of the mirror, three steps in each direction, front and back, and worried how many days she could maintain that look, given the paucity of her wardrobe.

She arrived at the Tribune office precisely six minutes before 8 o'clock. Her brisk walk through City Park had reminded her that her stomach was empty. "Ah, well, no time for breakfast," she had said to the pigeons gathered at the foot of the bandstand. Inside the main entrance she stopped at the receptionist's window. The older lady with glasses occupying the cubicle was not the same person who had been working there on her prior visits. Anne Marie introduced herself. "I'm reporting for work. This is my first day. I'm supposed to see Mister Lesnick," she said in crisp short sentences. "My name is Anne…"

"I know your name. Right here, on the ledger," said the receptionist. "Anne Marie Duboys, for the newsroom. Here are some forms you must fill out. You can use the desk behind me."

Anne Marie looked down at the nametag pinned to the receptionist's dark green sweater. "Excuse me, Mrs. Fournier, the name is Dubois, pronounced Doobou-ah, like in French."

"Well, that's fine and dandy."

"I think a person's last name is important. Would you like me to pronounce yours, Fourni-err or Fourni-ay?"

"Doesn't matter. It's not my name, it's my husband's. My maiden name is Gardiner, pronounced Gardnah, in the Maine tradition."

"I see."

"Look, young lady, just fill out the forms if you don't mind. Mister Lesnick should be here in a few minutes." Mrs. Fournier waved the new employee to the area behind the switchboard. "Newsroom, huh! Good luck with that," she mumbled.

As she headed for the desk, Anne Marie once again heard her mother's voice: "You did what? You did what?" She took her time, reading carefully the questions, scrolling through the three-page document. Near the end, she saw a paragraph with the heading 'Salary History.' The space was blank.

"Good morning, Miss Dubois."

"Good morning, sir,"

"Just routine questions," Mister Lesnick said. "Just routine paperwork. Take your time, and here's a pen, one of those new fandangle inventions called ballpoints. I'll be in the newsroom when you're ready."

"Thank you, sir." At the very top of the first page was a space set aside for a date. Anne Marie wrote: September 12, 1943.

Anne Marie tried to concentrate on the questions, but her attention easily wandered since her seat offered an open view of the front door to the newspaper office. As she would soon learn, Monday mornings were hectic, chaotic even.

"Morning, Laura," most of the arrivals tossed at the receptionist who barely acknowledged them. The phone was ringing constantly, and she displayed the versatility of a seasoned receptionist as she connected each caller to the right party and still managed to hand over to the reporters and clerks any slips of paper that awaited them in the many cubby-holes of the workstation.

Anne Marie thought the men looked scruffy. Hardly anyone wore a tie, many kept their hats on as they rushed into the newsroom. The one exception was a highly polished-looking chap, perhaps in his late 30s, who doffed his hat as he greeted the receptionist. He was about to go into the newsroom when he turned and, facing Anne Marie, said, "Laura, don't tell me they've given you an assistant, and such a pretty one at that."

"Mister McGraw, you know it's not my job to introduce you to new employees. Mister Lesnick will take care of that."

"Laura, don't tell me this pretty young thing is destined for the newsroom? Certainly, hope so," he said loudly as he stopped in front of Anne Marie. "Good, morning, my name is Aylrod McGraw. I'm on the sports desk over there. And you are…"

"Anne Marie Dubois."

"My, my, my, that sounds like a French movie star."

"Well, your name sounds like a Viking warrior's," she replied.

They both took a minute to flaunt wide smiles while shaking hands.

The receptionist shooed him away. Making sure he went to the ewsroom, she turned to Anne Marie. “Don’t pay him any mind; he’s so ıll of himself. Trouble in the trousers is what I call him.”

Anne Marie returned to the questionnaire, wondering about Laura’s emark and making a mental note about being careful not to confide too ıuch to the receptionist. Her eyes fixed on the blank section titled salary, he took a deep sigh, and whispered, “First things first.”

As she entered the newsroom Anne Marie was once again verwhelmed by the metallic noise of the typewriters, and the conveyor ack affixed to the ceiling and by the shrill sound of telephones.

Mister Lesnick signaled that she should join him in his office, a mall space with half-walls. “Sorry about the noise. I’m sure you’ll get sed to it.” He explained that Monday mornings were the most hectic – crazy” was the word he used, adding that since there was no Sunday dition, there was a lot of catching up to do. “The world doesn’t stop just ecause it’s Sunday.” He invited Anne Marie to sit down. “Let’s take a ook at this.” Quickly he perused the employment forms, checking off a ew items. On the final page, Mister Lesnick looked at his new employee. So, Miss Dubois, were you planning on asking me how much we will ay you?”

“Well,” she replied hurriedly, “the question has been on my ıind…”

“Starting pay is $37 a week, paid every other week. That would be check for $74. You will be salaried of course, so the hours on the job on’t affect your take-home pay. The work week is Monday through aturday. We’ll soon set up your daily schedule. Some of your expenses vill be reimbursed, but we’ll discuss that later. I imagine there won’t be ıany, at least not at first. There usually is a performance review after the rst month and there might be a salary adjustment at that time. Do you ave any questions?”

“No. So, I assume I start today.”

"That's the plan. I'll have someone give you the tour and you ca meet everybody. Did you bring a notepad?"

Anne Marie shook her head. "No, I didn't think of that."

"Not a problem. We have a closet full of supplies. And you ca keep that ballpoint pen."

The editor donned a sly smile. "The Obituary Girl, that could b your title. At the start of every week, we're overrun by funeral hom directors with obituaries. That will be your introduction; that's your des over there: the obituary desk."

Looking over her head, Mister Lesnick said, "Your tour guide ha just arrived. Let me introduce you."

He rose and Anne Marie followed his lead as a finely dresse woman in her 50s entered the cubicle. "Anne Marie Dubois, here is th associate society editor. She'll give you the grand tour."

"You can call me Miss O'Brien," the guide said as she extende her hand and smiled at her young charge. "So pleased to have you join u at The Great Falls Evening Tribune."

Anne Marie resisted the natural urge to curtsy and merely smiled i return. And the two ventured through the bustle of the newspaper office

THREE

FRENCH TOAST IN A GHETTO

Surrounding her on all sides, a group of women in blue dresses yell at her, spitting out their comments. Anne Marie is unable to resist the assaults, to respond, to escape. She is lies on her back on a narrow table covered with a white ruffled piece of cloth, her arms frozen at her side, her head immobile. Although her eyes are tightly closed, she can see her tormentors, she can identify her fellow residents.

The women send their barrage of nastiness:

- "You think you're so smart."

- "So, tell us again how great you were as a reporter."

- "You think you're so pretty."

- "You think you're the smartest one here."

Behind these women are nurses and attendants. They say nothing but their airs are those of agreement if not endorsement.

- "You have opinions on everything."

- "You look down on all of us."

Anne Marie feels a strong hand on her shoulder. A fresh voice repeats: "Miss Dubois, wake up. Wake up, please."

Slowly the shroud retreats, and the new voice soothes. "Here, Miss Dubois, let me help you up. Let's get you dressed. It's time for breakfast."

Anne Marie awakens and rubs her eyes, gazing at the smiling face of Julie, the young aide. "Oh my God. What a dream," she says as she struggles to get out of bed.

"Let me help you," offers Julie. "Lean on my shoulder. My, you seemed to be really deep in your dream. Hope it was a good one."

"Like a funeral without a coffin."

"Oh, my. That sounds horrible."

Anne Marie coughs several times, attempting to expel all memory. As her feet firmly hit the carpet, she catches her breath. "Julie, have you ever been to a wake, and you see everyone standing around the coffin and they are sharing anecdotes about the deceased?"

"Yes, of course."

"Did you ever wonder if the deceased could hear what was being said?"

Breakfast is Anne Marie's favorite meal. The mood is relaxed, the staff refreshed, and the food inviting. Her fellow suffragettes display openness to the day's possibilities, Anne Marie surmises, although she's had many opportunities to test that assumption and found it illusory. Yet, despite the grayness of this morning in February, there are smiles and nods and calmness among the dozen or so residents of Laura F. Washburn Home. Anne Marie sits alone as usual. She reads the menu card and orders her favorite: French toast with a side dish of canned pears and a cup of black coffee – the latter a habit she adopted decades before at the newspaper. She smiles as she recalls the look of astonishment on the faces of her fellow reporters the first time she poured herself a black coffee in the lunchroom. "My, my," everyone seemed to be saying, "coffee without milk or cream – that's not appropriate for a young lady." Anne Marie nods at a thin lady in a bright red housecoat sitting at the table next to hers. "Cheers," Anne Marie says and lifts her cup in a toast to the new day.

Sipping the strong coffee while waiting for her French toast, her memory journeys to those early days at the Tribune. She sees the faces of her fellow reporters, unsure of how to treat a young woman in the newsroom, unable to find a level of mutual interest, the exception being Aylrod, the assistant sports editor who had warmly greeted her on her first day at work. "Oh, he was so handsome, so debonair," she mutters, casting a hurried glance around the dining room to check if anyone has heard her, in part wishing someone had and hoping someone would ask whom she's referring to. That conversation, Anne Marie had rehearsed several times. "Who are you referring to?" Thus went the imaginary dialog. "Oh, just a fellow reporter. He was so dashing. His smile and his words were so inviting. He made me feel like I belonged."

"Ah, *merci beaucoup*," Anne Marie says to the cafeteria worker. "French toast deserves a convivial greeting in French." She pours a phony maple syrup on the pieces of fried bread and starts eating daintily. Aylrod still on her mind, she remembers that Sunday morning when she had accepted his invitation to breakfast at Nichol's Tea Room where she had ordered French toast and it had been served with real Vermont maple syrup. How she had wished the moment to last forever, but the bells of *Notre-Dame* Church pealed in the distance, and she knew her mother and brothers would be looking for her at Mass. Hurriedly walking to church, Anne Marie cherished Aylrod's goodbye: "We should do this more often." She closes her eyes and relives the episode, recalling how her mother was upset that Anne Marie had opted not to take Communion, how she couldn't tell her she hadn't fasted and had breakfast with her co-worker Aylrod.

Her reminiscence is interrupted when she hears a new voice, one far from endearing – that of Mrs. Wiggins.

"Good morning, Miss Dubois." She doesn't wait for Anne Marie's response. "I have someone here I would like you to meet. We have a new resident as of last night." Mrs. Wiggins takes a step back and, waves to summon a woman with long white hair and an eager smile, she then introduces her. "May she join you for breakfast?"

Anne Marie automatically pulls a chair back and offers a welcoming if uncertain nod.

"Miss Landry here also speaks French. Just like you do. I thought you two would have lots to share." Looking down at the breakfast plate she gushes, "And French toast, how appropriate."

Anne Marie takes a deep breath, and examines her new table companion, assuming she's just as uncomfortable as she is. "Welcome to the Washburn Home. I am Anne Marie Dubois. Please call me Anne Marie."

"I suggest you order quickly, the kitchen will be closing soon," offers Mrs. Wiggins.

"Excuse me, Mrs. Wiggins, but did I hear you correctly? Did you say, Miss…"

"Landry," interrupts the new resident. "Angie is my first name."

Anne Marie becomes focused. After a quick grin, she finishes her sentence. "Did you say she speaks French? Is that why you brought her to my table, Mrs. Wiggins? Are you trying to create a neat little ghetto here? Let us put all the French people at the same table, to keep them out of the way. Is that what you are doing?"

"Miss Dubois, your level of sarcasm is especially fine-tuned this morning…are you sure you're taking all your pills"?

Addressing her new table mate, Anne Marie says, "Sorry, Angie, ut I have learned that around here, you have to make your feelings nown, loud and clear."

Clearly confused, the newcomer proceeds to get up from the table. I'm sorry. Nobody asked me to do anything, I just followed her here…"

Anne Marie slumps into her seat. "I am the one who should be orry. I have behaved badly. Listen, let us have breakfast together." She ooks up at Mrs. Wiggins and gives her the fiercest look she can muster. Now Angie, if everybody can leave us alone, we will get acquainted. I o recommend the French toast; it is quite good."

A few minutes later, with the breakfast order in front of her, Angie ollects herself for a moment and whispers some words. Her eyes closed, he makes a sign of the cross, then looks up at Anne Marie and smiles.

"So, Miss Landry, where are you from?"

"Born and raised in Norridgewock, a small town near Skowhegan."

"Really…I have been up there a few times, wrote a story once about ne Jesuit priest who was killed by the British during the French and ndian wars."

"That was Father Rasle. He has a monument in Norridgewock."

"Yes, that is correct. I saw it on one of my trips. In the article, I vrote about the process of canonization of Father Rasle. I interviewed a ew people who were proposing his sainthood. That was in the mid-50s. remember talking to an old fellow who sounded so bitter. He was upset nat the Vatican had canonized the so-called North American Martyrs – ne Jesuit missionaries who worked with the Iroquois in New York State but refused to canonize Father Rasle. I remember he told me it was ok o make a saint out of someone who was killed by the Indians but not omeone killed by the English. I also remember that my editor had emoved that comment from my article, explaining it was too political."

"You worked as a writer? When and for whom?"

"I was a reporter – I suppose that is close to being a writer. I wa the first woman reporter at The Great Falls Evening Tribune, startin way, way back in the forties. I covered local court proceedings at first an then local politics and later I branched out into features."

"Oh, my…we have a celebrity here at Laura F. Washburn Hom What an honor!"

Anne Marie smiles. "I appreciate your comment, but Angie pleas do not make a big deal out of this; the other residents are not at a impressed."

"Well, Miss Dubois, don't tell anybody but I'm part Abenaki, o my mother's side. Her family was among the survivors of the Englis massacre; they escaped to Canada."

"Really, that makes YOU a celebrity."

"Maybe, but please don't tell anyone. I don't know how my India connection would be accepted here. They may think I'm looking to sca them."

The new friends laugh heavily at that remark.

After breakfast, the two continue their conversation as they walk their rooms. Angie, considerably shorter than Anne Marie and obvious younger, walks briskly, her lengthy locks swinging behind her. After few steps, she realizes her newfound friend is dragging behind and sh shortens her gait.

"I never worked in what I would call an intellectual setting – like newspaper," says Angie. "During high school, I worked at a convenienc store that also served as a bus depot on the Boston-Québec line and I g to meet many interesting people. The store was appropriately called 'Th Stop' and it was the focus of downtown Norridgewock. It had two larg signs in the window: Cold Drinks and Hot News." Anne Marie laug generously. "We carried a few newspapers – weeklies and few dailie But I preferred the magazine section of the store, especially th Hollywood gossip ones. That's where my boyfriend and I would hang o in the evenings when his shift was over. He worked in the print shop at the local weekly paper. Ah, Jerome was my date at my high school prom and my steady date for several months after graduation. Oh, I'm sorry, Anne Marie, boring you with all these details about my youth."

"Not at all, Angie. I love to hear people's stories. That was my favorite ingredient as a reporter. Go on, tell me more."

"Well, when the paper he worked for closed, Jerome moved to Portland and that was the end of our romance. I had just turned 20 and I loved him so…I would have married him, yes indeed."

"That is fascinating. We are so much alike, Angie. My first true love was a fellow reporter, but that did not last very long."

The two ladies slow their pace and continue walking in silence. Finally, Anne Marie asks, "Angie – that is a shortened version of what name?"

"Angélique."

"Really! That is so charming."

"But please, don't tell anyone. Angie is fine. I was raised as Angie, I spent most of my adult life as Angie. Angélique sounds so precious, so sanctimonious."

They stop at a room three doors down from Anne Marie's room. "Here I am. Angie's Place. Heh, heh, that's the name of a beer hall in the town of Madison. But that's another story, for another day."

"Well, I have a story to share with you about this room. As long as I have been here, it belonged to Doris. We all knew her as Doris, the Disco Queen. Her door was always open, and she was always dancing, listening to Donna Summer. She died a couple of weeks ago. Quite a blend here: Angélique, the Disco Queen!"

They chuckle and say goodbye, waving to each other as Anne Marie keeps walking to her room.

The next morning, Angie stands at the open door of her room. She looks up and down the corridor and sees no one. She listens to the indistinct sounds of the television set in the lounge and is tempted to go check for any other sign of life. "*Mon Dieu*, this is surely the waiting room at the morgue," she murmurs. A few minutes later, she spots Anne Marie emerging from her room at the end of the corridor. Angie waves enthusiastically to her. "Good morning, neighbor," she says.

"How are you, my dear?" Anne Marie sends the words down the hallway and regrets using the expression "my dear" thinking it's premature since she's known the younger resident barely a full day. "And, it sounds so pedantic," she says under her breath.

"Fine, I guess. But there's a dilemma lurking here. What do I do with these?" Angie asks as she takes a few steps back into her room. "There's no room in here, it's already so crowded." Next to her are three suitcases, two small ones and a larger one with a brown leather casing.

Anne Marie focuses on the large one, remembering a similar portmanteau that populated her youth. She moves close to it and, bending down slightly, strokes it dreamily. "My mother had one just like this. I remember it so well. It had a hidden pocket."

"I'm sure it's an antique. It was given to me by *Mère* Marie-Louise, the superior at the convent in Baie St-Paul."

"It's beautiful." Anne Marie wants to inquire about the suitcase. Why was it given to her? What was she doing at the convent? Why did she still have it? Did it have a secret pocket? "It is a treasure," is all she manages to say as she steps back into the hallway to absorb the scene: Angie is seemingly worried as she stands between the smaller suitcases and the large leather one. Suddenly, Anne Marie sees her mother standing there instead of Angie, wearing her winter coat and boots, her portmanteau at her feet, ready to leave their Blake Street apartment. Anne Marie closes her eyes, covers them, blinking, wiping them, wanting to banish the scene.

"Make sure to have them tagged with your name. The Home has plenty of room for luggage in the basement. It is dry and clean. They will be safe. All you have to do is go to the receptionist and ask for Tom. He will bring them down to the basement for you."

Without another word, Anne Marie rushes to her room down the hallway. She enters and heads straight for her little closet and the photos of her canaries. She no longer holds back the tears, she fully plunges into the painful vision of her mother leaving to attend her father's funeral. "Oh! My dear friends, you never knew about my Papa's funeral. That is something of my past I have never shared with you, my faithful canaries." She hears fragments of angry conversation from so many years ago. She drops into the small vanity seat Tom had rescued for her and pulls the heavy drape behind her to seal the seclusion. "My Papa left Great Falls to return to Canada when I was eleven years old. I never forgave him for abandoning us. Often, I asked my *Maman* why she had let him go. She simply said that he never felt like he belonged here. He was not made for a world of bricks and smokestacks, and neither could he bear the howls of the mill's whistle when the work shifts would change. *Maman* told me that Papa would constantly complain about living in crowded four-and-five-storied tenement buildings. He yearned for a rolling landscape where all one could see was a farmhouse, barns, and pastures. He confessed to my *Maman* that he craved the silence of the fields and the woods. He had enjoyed the rural routine, the felling of trees for firewood, growing vegetables for his kitchen table, and raising a variety of farm animals to feed and clothe the family. Papa never accepted the need to move to a mill town in Maine to bury himself under a pile of bricks. And when *pépére* died and left no one to care for the homestead that had been in the Dubois family for generations, my Papa went back to Saint-Césaire without hesitation. I heard these stories throughout my young years, yet we argued constantly, my *Maman* and I. Why did you allow him to leave you? Didn't you love each other? Why didn't you tell him he had a daughter here to care for? Oh, and whenever he came back for visits to Great Falls – usually at Christmas time – I refused to speak to him. And, when I was old enough to fully understand, I hated him further for what I considered the only reason for his visits: to make my *Maman* pregnant, to leave a baby boy in her stomach."

Anne Marie rubs the soreness of her neck. gazes at the varied mementos of her newspaper years lining a small patch of her closet and reaches for the photos of her three canaries. "Oh, my little ones. I have spared you from these confessions. Oh, Father, Son, and Holy Ghost, please forgive me. It was the sight, just a few minutes ago, of that large suitcase with Angie down the hall. That image of my *Maman* preparing herself for the trip to Saint-Césaire to attend the funeral assaulted me and threw me into a pit of self-pity. I know, I know, my little birds, I should know better. My Papa's death was many years ago. Today, at my age, there should be scant room for self-pity." Yet, she goes on with the retelling.

"I was in high school when my Papa died. A wave of conflicting emotions flooded my teenage mind: sadness to see my *Maman*'s tears, bitterness from my Papa's abandonment, and guilt for not accompanying my *Maman* to the funeral. She had explained that I needed to stay home to attend school, to take care of my brother. Finally, I told her to run off to bury my Papa. My last words: I hope his grave sprouts nothing but poisonous weeds."

Anne Marie rises from the seat in her tiny closet and pulls back the drape that defines the space. "Yes, indeed. At my age, no room for self-pity."

"Happy birthday to you, happy birthday to you…" A feeble choral refrain floats through Laura F. Washburn Home in honor of one of its occupants. It had been decided sometime before that the birth date of a resident was worth a celebration, its ingredients of song, pastries, and goodwill marking another year of life when the coming years seemed scarcer. On this day, the evening of the 4th of April, the group of ladies had gathered in the lounge to mark the birthday of Louise Fitzgerald. Nobody knows much about Louise, and what is known seems to be forgotten easily, but Mrs. Wiggins is thorough in her record keeping and she sees the birthday celebrations as an important part of her duties.

Angie and Anne Marie sit at a folding table in the large bay window that was the hallmark of what was now called the lounge.

"This was the original performance hall," explains Anne Marie. Once a month, the Central Maine Literary Society sponsored a concert ere. They favored performances by their own members of course. I overed a few of these in my early years at the newspaper; I thought they vere boring."

"When was that?"

"In the mid-40s – 1940s, not the 1840s" Both ladies laugh.

"How old *are* you?" Angie asks, emphasizing the word 'are.'

"My birthday is in June. I will be a grand old 83. And, how old are ou?"

"I just turned 75. Almost a full decade separates us. Can't you tell?" Both ladies laugh once more. "Well, I look forward to an afternoon tea to elebrate your birthday in June."

"Do not count on it. Last year hardly anyone came to my birthday vent. You know, I am not very popular here. I have no friends. In fact, ny dreams are filled with visions of something like a funeral. I dream I m lying on a table, and my fellow residents stand all around me and ronounce all kinds of mean-spirited allegations: 'You talk too loud, you nink you are so smart, you are such a snob.' The same dream again and gain. It used to trouble me, but now I do not care, and I usually avoid nese little gatherings of tea and crumpets."

Angie replies, "Well thank you for introducing me to the tea and rumpets affair."

"You are most welcome, my dear."

"And I will pray that your dreams become easier to bear."

Mrs. Wiggins, the hostess, rings a tiny dinner bell to call attention) the goings-on, asking everyone to join her in wishing a happy birthday) Louise Fitzgerald who is turning 85 on the 4th day of April. Everyone ɔins Mrs. Wiggins in repeating another chorus of the happy birthday itty.

A few moments later, as a tray of scones is being passed aroun Anne Marie turns to her partner and asks, "Angie, the other day I notice you say a prayer before your meal. That is a nice thing to do."

"It's a habit left over from the days I had a habit," Angie replies.

"Oh, are you telling me you wore a habit? Were you a nun? An yes, I remember now you said something about a nun giving you one your suitcases…"

Angie interrupts: "Yes, that was mother superior at Baie St-Paul Canada. I was a member of that community. *Les Filles de Ste-Alice*. W had a hospice there, a beautiful place on the banks of the Saint Lawren River."

"Really, that is fascinating."

"Well, I wouldn't call it that. It's simply my life."

"Tell me about it. Please do."

"I told you that my maternal ancestry is Native American, th Abenakis from Norridgewock. That was never a major part of my lif but when my great-aunt on my mother's side passed away a long tim ago, my mother convinced me to accompany her to the funeral in Canad in Chibougamau, Québec. There I met a couple of distant cousins wh were nuns, members of *Les Filles de Ste-Alice*. I had just turned 30 an Jerome, the love of my life, and I had parted ways. I think I told you abo that. So, the cousins in Chibougamau – I usually whisper that name, don't want anyone to think I'm throwing about Indian incantations– the took me in and, as they say, the rest is history."

"Fascinating, truly fascinating," Anne Marie repeats. "Tell me ho you wound up sitting here at Laura F. Washburn Home."

"Well, I made my vows at the convent in Chibougamau and I joine the staff at the local Catholic school as an English teacher. That laste almost 30 years. I participated fully in the life of the convent; I was on of the youngest nuns and the only American one. But I never acclimate to the landscape or the weather. Chibougamau is so far away, in Norther

Québec, in the middle of nowhere. It's a barren landscape, with hardly any forests, lots of lakes, an ice-covered half of the year, and the longest and harshest winters imaginable. Eventually, I was re-assigned to the *Hospice Ste-Alice* in Baie St-Paul hundreds of miles to the south, an area with milder winters and a more welcoming countryside. But I missed teaching and I found it difficult dealing with the elderly. And look at me now, I'm among the elderly that are hard to deal with!"

"So, Angie, you are now separated from the convents. Are you still a nun?"

"Yes and no. The community is practically non-existent – a very small number of very elderly sisters living in nursing homes like this one, scattered all over. I never renounced my vows, there was no one to renounce them to."

"I see." Anne Marie withdraws into quietness for several minutes, gazing at the budding apple trees on each side of the driveway.

"My faith is still very strong. I pray constantly. Every action is inspired by my religious training, but I miss a communal sense of life," Angie adds.

"I see, and I have wanted to ask you how you wound up here in Great Falls at this nursing home?" Anne Marie asks. "This is not a low-income retirement home, you know. How can an ex-nun afford this?" The question produces a period of silence in their corner of the room. "I am sorry...this is none of my business. I am so sorry. Please forgive me. And I am so sorry for the term 'ex-nun.' I should not speak this way."

Angie looks around her for several minutes. "Have you ever heard of the CFF? The initials refer to the Chamberland Family Foundation." Anne Marie replies that she hasn't and returns her gaze to the landscape outside.

"For over a hundred years, the Chamberland family has been the largest landowner in that part of the world...the thousands of acres on both sides of the Maine-Québec border. They've become a major contributor to the lumber industry, employing over a hundred workers on both sides of the border..." She stops suddenly as Mrs. Wiggins enters the old performance hall and announces that the residents should leave the room for the cleaning crew.

Anne Marie and Angie leave their table and follow the group out of the hall. Moments later, standing in the doorway to her room, Angie says: "The only reason I bring up the CFF is to answer your question. They are the ones who pay for my stay here."

"Oh...don't tell me you were also a lumberjack and you're using their retirement plan," Anne Marie offers with a smile.

"No, lumbering is not on my résumé. All I've ever chopped down were twigs around the convent. It seems that at some point, someone in the Chamberland family was educated by *Les Filles de Ste-Alice* on the Jackman side of the border and another member of the family was taken care of at *l'Hospice Ste-Alice* on the Canadian side. And, more recently, when the community of nuns saw itself on the point of disappearance, the CFF was contacted, and a fund was created to care for those nuns who moved to various nursing homes. And, here I am, and the rest is history!"

"Well, well, we really have a celebrity here," Anne Marie says with a gracious bow.

FOUR

DEADLINES A PLENTY

An unnatural silence had gripped the newsroom. Anne Marie was surprised. During her brief time at the Tribune, the newsroom was always a beehive of activity, but as she stepped into the room, the concentrated stillness shocked her.

She had spent the afternoon at the District Court where she felt increasingly confident in her understanding of the proceedings. That afternoon of November 22nd, 1943 had been filled with routine minor offenses. "Nothing to write home about," she muttered as she left the courtroom housed in the lower level of City Hall directly across the street from the Tribune. Anne Marie remembered, however, Ed Lesnick's comment when he had assigned her to the court beat. "Names, names, names, that's what sells newspapers. Names – for whatever reason, good or bad – that's what people want to read about, from birth notices to weddings, to obituaries, and everything in between."

"And who's scoring for the local sports teams, let's not forget," threw in Aylrod from the corner with the sports desks.

Everybody in the newsroom returned to reading the day's edition that had been printed much earlier than usual. Employees from other departments stood here and there holding copies of the paper. "Oh, my God," Anne Marie heard them say in muted tones. "Impossible," said one "What a tragedy!" stated another. "Those poor young boys, oh, my God."

Someone was sitting at Anne Marie's desk, and she hesitated, not knowing where to go when she caught Ed Lesnick's eyes. He nodded for her to come towards him. "No need to work on your court report. We've already gone to press. Here, read this." He handed her a copy of the paper as she sank into the chair facing him.

"Heavy casualties for U.S. forces in the Pacific."

The headline, in the boldest letters, stretched across the entire front page. Beneath it was a large photo of the battle scene. Anne Marie read the headline again. She took a deep breath and ventured into the body of the article about the Battle of Tarawa, a battle for control of an atoll in the Pacific Ocean. Early casualty reports for both the US Marines and the Navy were massive.

"The number killed and wounded will certainly surpass those of Guadalcanal," stated George Winslow, the veteran newsman and self-proclaimed expert on World War II.

"I certainly hope not," said one of the pressmen.

"Don't forget, Guadalcanal went on for six months. This is only from the second day of fighting for Tarawa," George replied.

Miss O'Brien from the social desk muttered, "I just pray none of our local boys were killed."

"Well, that's what happens in a war, people get killed. Whether from your town or the town next door, young soldiers get killed," George Winslow threw in.

“Ok. Ok. Everyone, calm down. We’ll see what happens omorrow,” stated Lesnick.

At that point, someone from circulation entered the room and asked anyone could help with the paper boys. “I’ve told them to be here early, nd we’ve printed extra papers for them to sell.” Anne Marie was the only ne to answer the call. She started walking towards the circulation epartment, the noises of war fading behind her.

Three days later, a woman cautiously walked into the newsroom at time when most of the crew was out on assignment. Standing in the oorway, she calmly introduced herself. “My name is Simone Charest nd I have a telegram from…” – she looked at the paper in her hand – from the adjutant general. It’s about my oldest boy, Arthur. He’s in the Marines. I think he’s dead.”

A couple of reporters looked up and one of them went to the editor’s ubicle. “There’s a lady here who says her son was killed in the war.”

Lesnick stood up and invited the woman to sit in his office. “I’m so orry. Let me see what you have there.”

As Mrs. Charest handed the telegram to the editor, she started obbing. “He’s my oldest. I have six other children at home, all very oung.”

“The Secretary of War desires me to express his deep regret that our son Arthur P. Charest has been killed in action on the Twenty-third Day of November 1943, in the Battle of Tarawa Atoll in the Pacific Theater. You will be promptly notified as to when his body will be elivered to you.
– Richmond Hill, Acting Adjutant General.”

Silence followed the reading. “I’m so sorry. So sorry,” offered the ditor.

"What do I do now? This has never happened before. My husbar is at work. He's going crazy because of this."

The newsroom editor advised her to retain a funeral director. "I' sure you must know someone." He stood up just as Anne Marie w returning from District Court. He motioned to her that she should jo him. "Here's Miss Dubois; she'll take you to our employee lounge whe you can catch your breath," he said to the grieving mother.

An hour later, Anne Marie came down to the newsroom a reported that Mrs. Charest's sister had joined her and that they had call the Bergeron Funeral Home. They were on their way to the funeral hom and Mrs. Charest's husband would join them there, Anne Mar elaborated further. "You know, Mister Lesnick, I've never done th before. How do you handle a grieving mother, what do you say? suggested she talk to Father Ouellet at *Notre-Dame* Church."

"There's not much one can say in this situation, but I'm sure yo helped," Lesnick stated. "Glad to have you on board, Miss Dubois. Th best obituary girl on staff," he said with a grin. "In any case, the new must go out. The undertaker's name is Bergeron, did you say? I shou call him, to make sure we're on the same page. I'll tell the wire edit about this. Gee, it's already noontime. I hope we can get the obituary today's edition."

Torn between sympathy for the Charest family and astonishment the editor's comments, Anne Marie rushed to her desk and buried herse in the minutiae of the day's court proceedings. "Life goes on at the dai newspaper, I suppose."

The next day – Thanksgiving – saw no edition. Everyone had th day off and took part in the traditional family gatherings enshrined American lore.

Early on Friday, November 26, a second local boy was reporte killed in action in the Battle of Tarawa. This time, no forlorn parent can to the newsroom with a telegram. Bradford Hodgkins, the owner Hodgkins Funeral Home, personally delivered a highly polished obitua of Thomas R. Goodwin of the US Marine Corps.

The Great Falls Tribune carried a front-page article about the death of Private Goodwin, a wide black border framing the obituary in contrast with the modest obituary of Private Charest tucked on page four a few days earlier.

Neither obituary included any details about funerals since nobody was sure when the bodies would reach Great Falls.

"I don't understand this," said Anne Marie's mother. "Who is this kid? How does he deserve this huge obituary on page one? And look at the size of that black border. You'd think he was FDR or someone like that. You know, lots of local boys have died in this war. Their obituaries didn't show up on page one like this. What makes him so special? I just don't get it. Anne Marie, can you explain it to me?" That evening, *Maman* Dubois had picked up the newspaper according to her usual routine and spent several minutes skimming it, while sitting in the rocking chair of her small kitchen. The Thanksgiving leftovers were warming in the oven and Anne Marie was setting the table. Her mother read the Goodwin boy's obituary twice and became quite agitated. She started her tirade in a loud voice, her words constantly interrupted by her son who kept asking when supper would be ready.

"And what in tarnation is an atoll?"

"I think it's a small rocky island."

"So, these boys gave up their lives for a pile of rocks somewhere in the Pacific. What a waste." *Maman* Dubois repeated her frustration over the Tribune's handling of the obituary. "The same battle at the same place on the same day. What really irritates me is that someone decided to put the obituary of the Charest boy way inside with a tiny headline that didn't even have his name. That's just not fair. How does that happen? Is the newspaper saying that one dead soldier is worth more attention than the other? Can you explain this to me?" she asked again.

"Shush, shush. We'll talk about it later," said Anne Marie, acknowledging to herself that she had no explanation. "*Maman*, let me find out what I can. Don't do anything rash. Let me get back to you before you run off and call an emergency meeting of *Les Dames Patronesses*.

Okay, *Maman*? Right now, my brother must be hungry, and supper must be ready."

Anne Marie also felt belittled by the placing of the obituaries. She knew the Charest obituary was rushed. Nobody in the Charest family seemed to know what to say about their son and brother. It compared very poorly with the Goodwin obituary which carried all kinds of references to the family's status in town, including references to the Goodwin Law Firm composed of the deceased boy's father and two uncles.

Anne Marie went to bed hoping that the next day would be much calmer at the newspaper. Could she – or would she – inquire about the placement of the two obituaries, she kept wondering.

Saturdays at the paper were usually low-key, with city hall and the district court closed for the weekend. It was a shopping day in Great Falls and the only hubbub could be found downtown. That Saturday, the newsroom happened to be short-staffed since most of the senior newsmen were stretching the Thanksgiving holiday into the weekend.

Normalcy, however, didn't make its appearance. The wire service was humming with the latest details on the Battle of Tarawa which had lasted only three days yet produced a victory for American forces. Two articles, both placed on page one, carried detailed reports on the battle involving both the Marine Corps and the Navy resulting in casualties of over 3,400. Anne Marie sat at her desk answering phone calls from residents whose sons were serving in the Pacific. She read some of the battle details to the callers and kept repeating that so far, the paper had been informed of only two deaths from Great Falls.

She was irritated by the chatter of her colleagues who read aloud the articles – especially Aylrod of the sports desk who gave the event a play-by-play slant. She wanted to tell him to tone it down, that this wasn't a sports event.

"You'd think we just went to war. Everyone's forgotten about the attack on Pearl Harbor and the battles all over Europe," Ed Lesnick said. He turned to his youngest employee: "Anne Marie, just tell people on the phone that military officials will be the ones to inform the family if anything happened. And don't tell them to listen to the radio. Tell them to read the paper."

"Yes, Mister Lesnick," she replied.

He motioned her to approach him at his desk. "As much as this can be irritating, the publisher has decided we need more ways to get people's reactions. He says we need more articles, not less. So, I'd like you to get some feedback from the community. We're shorthanded; I have no one else. So, I'd like you to go downtown and talk to people. There should be lots of people out. I'm sure this is what they're all talking about. Try staking out Graham's Department store. That's familiar territory…"

"Mister Lesnick, I...uh I'm not sure I…eh," she said falteringly.

"Well, maybe not Graham's. But anywhere. Just talk to people. See how people feel. Try to get quotes and names as much as possible. Remember, names, names, names."

Anne Marie nodded. She stood and started putting on her winter coat.

"And, Anne Marie, how long have you been working here?"

She hesitated, not knowing where the query was leading. "A bit over two months," she replied, fearing some kind of reproach.

"Well, you can start calling me Ed. No more Mister Lesnick. Okay? Now get going and be back by 11 o'clock."

Due to the November wind, Anne Marie decided she wouldn't stand on a corner with pad and pencil hoping to get folks to talk to her. She headed for Woolworths' Five and Dime where she knew the lunch counter would be hectic with a late breakfast crowd. That turned out to be a good decision, but the comments, although numerous, were very similar, and many of the people she spoke to would not allow her to use their names. On the way back to the newspaper office, she noticed that the Great Falls Hardware store was having a sale. "Early Winter Sale starts today" stated an enormous sign over the front door. She went inside and found a willing and eager assemblage of men of all ages with opinions to share and pleased as punch to be quoted. More than one of them aske her, "Do you really work at the paper?" and she proudly showed he credentials – a neatly folded paper Ed Lesnick had given her when sh first started work.

Proud of the article that resulted from her foray downtown, Ann Marie occupied *Maman's* rocking chair that evening and read it out lou to her brother André. "See, it has my byline," she proudly said.

"What's a byline?" he asked her.

"It's an attribution."

"What's that?"

"The name of the writer, in dark letters between the headline an the article itself," Anne Marie explained.

Her mother leaned over and examined the back page item. "Let m see: "A.M. Dubois. Huh, I hadn't noticed that. That's the first time, isn' it?"

"Yes, it is," Anne Marie said with a wide smile.

"Why not your full name? Why just the initials A and M?"

"I didn't ask. Maybe Mister Lesnick isn't ready to announce to th world that The Great Falls Evening Tribune has a female reporter."

"Well, one thing at a time," said her *Maman*.

In the middle of the following week, the bodies of Private Goodwi and Private Charest arrived in Great Falls and the funeral home director provided details about the funeral services. Another local family was als advised that their son, a member of the Marine Corps as well, had bee severely injured and was hospitalized in Hawaii.

Readers' attention focused on the two local boys who had given ieir lives fighting the Japanese. The partners in the Goodwin Law Firm the father and two uncles of the deceased – were the most vociferous, sking in a letter to the editor what kind of public ceremony would be eld in addition to the funeral service. The letter reminded everyone that ie grandfather, Albert J. Goodwin, had been a long-serving member of ie City Council back in the twenties and had been a Republican andidate for the Maine Legislature.

"Ok. The loss of a young man in a war is always a tragedy," stated d Lesnick. "But the Goodwin boy is not alone. Not this time, and ertainly not since World War II started." George Winslow chimed in. According to my count, we've had thirty-seven boys from Great Falls se their lives. That's my official count. All these lads were given proper unerals with military escorts. Not one was singled out in a special eremony." Nobody in the newsroom dared contradict Winslow who saw imself as the resident authority on the war and no one wanted to argue ith him. "It's obvious to me that the Goodwins are using this to advance ieir own agenda."

Someone noted that the timing was awkward. "We're already in ecember. This could interfere with the Christmas shopping season. It ould affect advertising."

"Well let's keep all of that to ourselves. We don't make the ecisions anyway. If the Mayor and City Council want a special eremony, they'll have it and all we can do is report on it," Lesnick said his staff.

It was late afternoon and the day's edition had already come out. s always, everyone was reviewing the newspaper and commenting on ie content. Anne Marie just listened, not confident enough to take part the discussion. She made mental notes and used the comments to crease her familiarity with Great Falls, its politics, its institutions, and s economy.

"Hey guys, you know what I came upon this afternoon. While lking to a few sports fanatics at the arena, I found out that both these boys were on their respective schools' hockey teams, and they playe often against each other." Everyone turned to stare at Aylrod on the spor desk.

"That's interesting," offered the editor. "Neither obituai mentioned that."

"I can see the headline now: Opponents on the ice united in dea in the Pacific," said Winslow. Everyone nodded their agreement. The da was over; the reporters cleared their desks and headed for the employe lounge and to their cars, traveling back to their homes for the evenir meal.

"I have an assignment for you." That was how Ed Lesnick greet his latest employee on the morning of December 2nd. His tone seeme hesitant, Anne Marie thought. The editor explained that the placing of tl two soldiers' obituaries the previous week had been criticized by son French people in town. "Father Ouellet and a couple of the merchants Omer Labadie, owner of the bakery, and Jules Goudreau, who runs tl brickyard – have accused the newspaper of favoritism. And you are awa of the letter to the editor from the lawyers, asking if Great Falls was goir to hold a public memorial for the Goodwin boy. Well, the powers that t upstairs, the Editorial Board members, want us to do something speci for both soldiers – to level the playing field, so to speak."

The young reporter had never seen her editor this upset. As sl listened to him rant on and on, she wondered what he thought she cou do about the situation.

"So last night I was thinking about all of this and I remember what Aylrod said yesterday about both kids being hockey player And…an idea came to me. We need one article about each boy, side t side, that displays them as regular high school kids, and shows that eac in his own way is a hero."

Anne Marie starts fidgeting, laying her coat on one side of her lap and then on the other. "You don't want me to write these articles, do you? Why not Aylrod?"

Ed took a deep breath. "Listen, Anne Marie, your article last week about local ordinary folks and their reaction to the battle was well done, and well received. Even the publisher mentioned it to me. Let's see if we can come up with something as good that focuses on the lives of the two lads. The wakes start today. I've talked to both funeral homes about my idea and they've agreed to help us out. They're expecting you this afternoon. The Bergeron Funeral Home and the Hodgkins Funeral Home are located on Pine Street, practically facing each other. I suspect this evening would be the best time. Family and friends will all be there. Just go and observe. Talk to people. Tell them you're with the paper. If they ask, say you're thinking of writing an article. If you think you will quote individuals, tell them you might do that and ask their permission. You know, like you did at Woolworth's and the hardware store last week. Take plenty of notes, and we'll review what you've got tomorrow. And I've asked Aylrod to work on something pertaining to the hockey teams. And I've asked him to help you with your assignment. If, of course, you think it necessary."

A long moment of silence punctuated his remarks. Anne Marie sighed and finally stood. "Don't worry about any other news. This is your only assignment for the next few days. Ok, Anne Marie?"

It wasn't a question and Anne Marie knew it.

She opted to visit the Charest family first, being more familiar with the Bergeron Funeral Home due to the many wakes for family, friends, and neighbors held there over the years. The smallish yet formal brown clapboard house was a strong part of the community – Anne Marie's community.

After an hour or so with the Charest family, she walked to the Hodgkins Funeral Home several yards up the street, on the elevated side of Pine Street where the Goodwin wake was being held. Here was a much more imposing brick building with a Victorian tower on the South corner. Anne Marie had walked past it countless times but had never entered.

Later that evening, Anne Marie walked home in a panic in her step. The wind was howling, and a fringe of snow lined the lonely sidewalks, but the panic she felt went beyond the early December weather. How could she write these articles about the dead boys? How could she translate her uncertainty into something readable for the general public?

In her tiny bedroom, she propped herself up and read her notes again and again. She had described each of the funeral homes, the families of the dead soldiers, and other visitors, and jotted down some of their comments.

Mrs. Charest greets her with a thin smile and introduces her to her husband Armand who's standing next to his son's casket. Two of Private Charest's brothers, both in their early teens, accompany their father like posted guards. They stare at the small, framed photograph of the deceased atop the closed casket. The room overflows with family and neighbors. Mrs. Charest doesn't stay still, running around comforting the older folks and reprimanding the very young. Anne Marie copied some of her words:

"Sorry about the noise. There are a lot of children in the family, with Ernest's brothers and sisters and all the cousins. I tried to find some sitters, but everyone wanted to be here. The very young ones don't understand what's going on. Father Ouellet said prayers, but the kids didn't pay attention. In church, they know to be quiet, but not here."

A man in a brown habit identified himself as Brother Jacques, Arthur's homeroom teacher at Saint-Antoine High School.

"He excelled in civics and geography. That lad was so fascinated by the Crusades. He told me once he wished he lived during those days, he would have gone to Jerusalem to liberate it from the Muslims. He wasn't among the top students in the class. But he was attentive."

An uncle was talking to a group of men in one corner of the room. He seemed to know the soldier well and was telling all kinds of tales about his playing sports, especially hockey.

"He was a terrific skater, but not very fast. Not fast enough for hockey and he never really excelled at the sport, although he was dependable. You know it's a small school and the teams have to work with what they've got. I was there when he made a real smart goal once, and everybody cheered his name 'Ti-tur, Ti-tur, Ti-tur.' That was his nickname. Little Arthur."

During one relatively quiet moment, Mrs. Charest approached Anne Marie.

"You know, I had a feeling my Arthur wouldn't come back. He wasn't drafted, you know. He was too young to be drafted. He enlisted. I was the first one he told. Not even his father. I asked him why he enlisted. He said he wanted to see the world, but I knew his real reason was to escape from taking over his father's business – you know Charest's Shoe Repair. Everyone knew that Arthur was destined to take over the family business. I guess, he figured he might as well go into the Marines and learn new things and see new places before having to spend his life as a cobbler in a Maine mill town."

"Are you ok? Hope you can get some sleep." Her mother said on the other side of the bedroom door. "There's always tomorrow to deal with your assignment. Turn off the light and get some rest." Welcoming the interruption, Anne Marie obeyed and put away her notes. "The Goodwin notes will have to wait," she told herself, fully aware that her night would stay on the edge of sleep.

Anne Marie woke up early the next morning and escaped downtown to Nichol's Tea Room where she ordered her usual breakfast; One-eyed Jack, the menu called it: a single fried egg sitting on Rye toast,

and a cup of black coffee. Her favorite table, discretely positioned at th
rear, next to the kitchen, gave her a comforting amount of privacy, ye
offered a good view of the comings and goings of the early mornin
customers, an array of store clerks, and office workers.

Her visit to the Hodgkins Funeral Home the evening before ha
seemed very formal. She remembered being greeted by the owner wh
drily warned her that she should be discreet and respect anyone attendin
the wake – even if they refused to speak to her.

Anne Marie opened her folder and scanned the page.

"A dozen people. All adults, many elderly. Everyone speaking in
low voice, or not at all. No children. Well-dressed folks in twos or three
would come into the formal room, neglecting to pay homage to th
deceased, and head directly towards the owners of the law firm, to expres
their feelings of sympathy. It was all very brief and formal, and each visi
lasted but a few minutes."

She recognized a number of these visitors from the court session
she had covered. Others were familiar figures at City Hall. A balding ma
in his 70s walked up to her.

"You must be from the Tribune. My name is James T. Goodwin.
am an uncle of the deceased. I'm the oldest partner in the family law firm
Private Goodwin, my nephew, was a good boy, an honest boy. He was
great athlete, a member of the Turner High School hockey team. He wa
not especially interested in public affairs. His father – that's him sittin
over there – had high hopes for the boy. We all did. Please, make this fast
We know why you're here. Make it fast."

Anne Marie went up to the casket. It also was closed and displaye
a large colored photograph of Private Goodwin in his hockey uniform an
a photograph of a sports trophy. A well-dressed woman was standin
among the several floral bouquets and wreaths surrounding the casket.

"That photograph does not do him justice. He was truly a handsom
lad. I was his babysitter. I lived next door, and his mother recruited m
when I was in high school. His parents were often away. They had

ɔing-away party when he enlisted in the Marines, and I was invited. His ather was not there; he was working on a legal case in Portland that ɔparently went late. His father was not pleased that Tommy had enlisted. was told they had a serious battle over that and that one of his uncles ad intervened. Tommy was accepted at Bates College. I'm sure his ather played a role in that, but I suspect that Tommy was not interested living at home and going to the local college. He told me once he anted to see the world. Well, he did. Not the right part of the world, and ertainly not at the right time."

Anne Marie had added a couple of paragraphs, quickly jotting the ords down, unsure if any of it would be part of her article: A group of igh school students arrived. There were five of them, three boys and two irls. After paying their respects at the casket, they gathered in a far corner f the ornate viewing room, seemingly avoiding contact with members of e Goodwin family. Anne Marie waited a few minutes and walked wards the students. The Goodwin uncle blocked her and addressed the oup of young people. "Evening. Thanks for coming," he said. "We ɔpreciate it, but I'm going to ask you to leave now. We will start a prayer ervice and it's for the family only." He glanced at his brother lawyers ho nodded approval. A few minutes later, Mayor Deschambeau came to the room and was headed towards the Goodwin lawyers when he ɔotted me. "You work for the newspaper, don't you? What are you doing ere?" I tried to tell him I was on assignment. "The Tribune has done nough to turn this into a political event. This wake is a private affair. I ould expect you to leave immediately, young lady." I grabbed my coat nd left the funeral home. The classmates of Private Goodwin were still n the sidewalk chatting away. I was tempted to interview them but idn't.

"Good morning. My, aren't we early today." Anne Marie looked raight into Aylrod's eyes, and for a moment felt guilty. "I didn't know needed your permission to have an early breakfast at Nichol's Tea

Room," she replied, punctuating her comment with an expansive smil
She closed her notepad and crossed her hands over it.

"May I join you?" Aylrod asked. "It'd be a pleasure to start my da
having coffee with you. What is that? What are you working on, Ann
Marie?"

"Oh, well. Some notes I took at the funeral homes last night."

"I see…the funeral homes…eh…the funeral homes?"

"Yes. The Charest boy and the Goodwin boy," Anne Marie replie
"You know, the Marine casualties. Their funerals are tomorrow. M
Lesnick – I mean Ed – assigned me to do a write-up about the wakes. An
he told me you would be contributing an article about the boys' being c
their high school hockey teams and that you would be helping me wi
my article. Didn't he tell you?"

Aylrod hesitated; he scanned the eatery looking for a waitres
"You're right. Ed did say something about the hockey connection. I'
forgotten. And, frankly, I hope he has too. It's a stupid idea."

There was silence in the corner of the eatery. Anne Marie push
her empty plate away and stared into her near-empty cup of coffe
"Where is that waitress?" she asked under her breath. She looked
Aylrod. "So, you're not going to help me? That's what Ed said."

"I'm not sure what he meant. How can I help you? You're a goo
reporter," he offered. "I've read your stuff." He patted Anne Marie on th
shoulder, allowing his hand to linger. He gave her a broad smile. "A
c'mon."

"I've never written anything like this. This has become so persona
so penetrating. It's like I'm writing a college paper about sociology an
culture…the way of life, the values of these people. Nobody has praise
the bravery, the patriotism of these boys. It's like these boys are using th
war and their military service as an escape. As I reread my notes, th
could be interpreted as a pacifist diatribe, an anti-war speech. It's not lik
anything I've ever seen in the Tribune, and I've been reading it since

was eleven years old. I just don't know...And I'm sure Ed said today's the deadline; he wants the article – or articles – today."

The waitress provided the necessary pause as she took Aylrod's order and refilled Anne Marie's cup of coffee.

"Well, let me see your notes." Aylrod looked at his watch. "We have about 20 minutes. And, if we're late, I'll tell Ed we were working on your article. And that will be the truth. Never mind that I was having breakfast with the prettiest newspaper reporter in the whole world."

Anne Marie didn't reply. She opened her notepad and pushed it towards Aylrod, all the time feeling her body temperature rise, attributing it to her refreshed cup of coffee.

At the restaurant exit moments later, Aylrod gallantly held the coat for Anne Marie so she could slip into it. Smiling, he opened the door for her and bowed to indicate she should step onto the sidewalk ahead of him. His gentlemanly ways backfired, and Anne Marie yelled out, "Oh, no!" when she stepped on a small patch of ice and nearly lost her balance. Reaching out to him to steady herself, Anne Marie found her arm laced around his. "Thank you, thank you Aylrod." Only when they rounded the corner on Park Street and faced the newspaper office did the duo disengage to walk into the employee entrance.

"So, what happens now?" she asked.

"Let's see if we can get a meeting with Ed. Let me do the talking."

Anne Marie went straight to her desk to check on any possible assignments for the day. A few minutes later, Aylrod was at her desk. "Do you mind if I share your notes with Ed?" She nodded, gave him her notepad, and pushed her chair back as if to get up. "Eh, I think Ed wants to go up to the publisher's office – both of us, he and I, that is."

She nodded and watched them leave the room. "I see. This is men's stuff."

Exactly 30 minutes later – Anne Marie had kept her eye on the master clock – Aylrod walked in and headed to the sports desk. In passing, he gave her a wink and a smile. A bit later, Ed Lesnick showed up. Then, nothing. Anne Marie waited a while, then started to leave the office to tour City Hall, her non-court day routine. She had her coat on and was nearly outside when Ed called her. "Do you have a minute, Anne Marie?" She knew it wasn't a question and took a position across from his desk.

"I see the mayor was at the wake for the Goodwin boy."

"Yes, he was not happy to see me there; he said the newspaper has done enough to politicize the deaths of the two boys. I didn't respond. And, when he told me to leave the funeral home, I did just that."

"Right move there, Anne Marie. No one's looking for a fight with City Hall."

"Listen. No decision's been made. The publisher has your notes. By the way, the notes are interesting, well done, they say a lot about the situation, and how each family is reacting to the tragedy of their loss. I told the publisher that this double funeral article isn't what we should be running with. We've printed enough about Tarawa. I strongly suggested we move on."

"The publisher didn't indicate what his decision would be, but since he didn't fly into a fit and didn't insist on getting his way, I strongly suspect the issue is dead – no pun intended." Ed smiled. "Now, go do your rounds. I'm sure there's something at the police station or fire station we can use in today's edition."

Anne Marie hesitated. "Thank you, Mister Lesnick...I mean Ed.

FIVE

SECRETS OF THE CEMETERY

Anne Marie had walked by the newspaper office hundreds of times without noticing the window boxes and their assorted blossoms, but in the waking spring months of her second year at The Great Falls Evening Tribune, she was amazed by the pansies and daffodils sprouting from the boxes that lined that section of Park Street. "I guess I was too busy in those days reading the headline banners taped inside the windows. Now, I can go in and be part of the news, instead of simply harvesting hints of the days' stories from the street." That was how she explained the absence of the flower boxes in her memory. What she didn't voice was how the flowers symbolized the loveliness of spring love. That heart-warming feeling wasn't the sole result of bright sunshine and mild temperatures across the land. Her nascent relationship with Aylrod – her "mentor" as Ed described him – also played a role. All of a sudden, Anne Marie was fascinated by the sports world since Aylrod suggested she accompany him to a hockey game, a basketball game, or a baseball tryout. The morning after a sporting event they usually met for breakfast at Nichol's Tea Room to review the game. Aylrod was as charming as ever and he dispelled from Anne Marie's memory her first day at the paper when the receptionist had called him "trouble in th trousers."

Anne Marie remembered when, with her first paycheck in hand, sh returned to Graham's Department Store to purchase wardrobe items selecting a few pieces that would make her seem more mature an sophisticated. Her *Maman* had noticed the change, accepting it as a sig that her daughter was now in the public eye.

On the last Saturday of April, Anne Marie stopped at the newspape entrance and stretched forward and upward to pick a couple of youn tulips from the window boxes. She had brought a vase from her *Maman*' closet and planned on displaying the small bouquet on her desk in th newsroom. The window box was higher than expected and she lost he balance and dropped the vase onto the sidewalk. At that moment, Aylro arrived and said, "Anne Marie dear, are you picking those flowers for me How sweet."

For two days and nights, the skies had poured torrential rain ove Central Maine and easily convinced the layers of snow and ice on th mountainsides to join its downward flow into the streams and rivers an eventually into the bays of the Atlantic. "Not unusual for this time o year" George Winslow had offered, the dean of the newsroom.

On her way to work that Saturday morning, Anne Marie had wade through puddles, thanking her *Maman* who had insisted she wear tal boots. When she dropped the vase in her effort to pick the flowers, th water trapped beneath the window boxes had given the small urn a sof landing. Aylrod picked up the vase and commented on how elegant an stylish it was. "Just like you, my dear."

"Oh, thank you, how sweet," she responded with a big smile. Sh surprised herself as she formed her mouth into the shape of a kiss and sen it in his direction.

Inside the newsroom, after the customary 'good mornings' to th news crew, the duo headed for their respective desks and burie themselves in notes and memos connecting them to the job at hand. Hal an hour later, Ed announced that the wire service had provided th ribune with its banner story for the Saturday edition: overnight, the eavy rains had produced flooding along Maine's waterways, and in ome places, major landslides occurred. "Great Falls is the site of one of e largest landslides and police and emergency vehicles are on their way the landslide area, a section of the Mount Durham Cemetery that sits ose to the raging Amanusook River," Ed said. The newsroom staff, ways slimmer on a Saturday morning, responded with amazement.

"George, I am assigning you to cover the story. The photo epartment is also responding. Oh, and George, you better take Anne larie with you. Whatever the two of you had planned for today, put it side. This is a priority," Ed declared.

George responded, "You sure, Ed? The oldest and youngest embers of the staff?"

"I'm sure. You've got the experience and Anne Marie has a fine ye for detail. And, she doesn't have her driver's license yet. So, get oing, the two of you. This is going to be major, with other media all over ew England picking up our story."

Without further discussion, the two reporters started getting ready nd in a few moments were out of the newsroom. Aylrod stood and sent questioning look toward the editorial desk which Ed ignored.

The drive to the site took about 20 minutes. George dictated how e two would divide the task of covering the event. "I'll deal with the ops and other officials, you scan the area, and get a sense of the evastation."

Anne Marie nodded. She was somewhat familiar with the ndscape, having explored it with her high school group. The cemetery as erected on a hill, with the southern end directly on the river's edge. he anticipated that would be where the landslide occurred, the older ction of the cemetery being on lower land bordering the road. She membered that Mount Durham Cemetery was one of the oldest in the ea, having been part of a colonial-period congregation whose church ad burned down a long time ago. Her high school history teacher aimed there were graves there, of slaves owned by local farmers. The students were charged with reading the gravestones to see if any mig give clues about the slave trade. They spent several afternoons stompi around the simple markers, most of them having sunk into the ground, t students trying to decipher whatever markings were left. One section the cemetery was much more impressive with large monuments a statuary, many from the Civil War era. Officially, the cemetery w abandoned and unkempt, the county historical association having be given the deeds and the land. Anne Marie had been fascinated by the pla as a student. More than once, she had driven her bicycle there all alone explore it further. "It was so peaceful," she whispered as she and Geor Winslow arrived.

The scene was one of chaos. The reporters were soon informed th the hillside had collapsed and in the rubble were a few skeletons. "Son of the skeletons were evidently carried off by the swift curren announced the state police captain. "We found some bodies downstrea but at the water's edge in the dirt's debris were four more," he state adding that a state forensic expert was expected on the scene with a cre

"Did you find any caskets?" George asked. "Not yet," respond the state police captain. "That would indicate the caskets had rotted ov the years, or there were none. It could mean the area was a common bur ground, with the bodies simply dumped there."

"Can we quote you on that?" asked Anne Marie.

"No, you may not quote me. You can quote me on finding t skeletons, not a common burial ground." The captain added that poli headquarters would probably release a comprehensive report, but th would take a couple of days, maybe longer since this was a weekend.

The newspaper photographer caught up with the reporters. He to them he had climbed above the landfall and taken several shots, includi a few with skeletons and bones scattered all over the place. "Thanks, b I don't think we'll use the skeleton shots. We don't want the paper to lo like scenes from a horror film," said the older reporter.

At the office, Anne Marie wrote a detailed description of the si adding what she knew about the cemetery from her excursions there a fe years before, while George wrote about who was there responding to the emergency, including, almost as if in passing, a few quotes about skeletons.

Ed went to Anne Marie's desk at one point and offered, "You should check our morgue upstairs. You might find some reference works from the county historical society about this cemetery."

"The morgue… what morgue?" she asked.

"Oh, that's what we call the room on the top floor where we keep archives of the newspaper company and bound volumes of all the years we've been publishing, plus a library of reference materials. By the way, that is where your notes about the wakes for the casualties from the Battle of Tarawa can be found. In a file called 'Not fit to Print.'"

"I wondered why you didn't give them back to me."

"As far as today's story goes," Ed added. "Just give me a brief overview of the scene, describing its general location, without the historical background. That can come in a follow-up article, once you've researched it. Oh, and today's article is on page one with a double byline. And the other Maine dailies will also carry it…with the double byline. So, young lady, you're on your way to fame."

Anne Marie wasn't impressed or amused. She was totally depressed. The idea of skeletons being tossed about and thrown downhill into the muddy river remained with her for the rest of the day.

Exactly one week following the flood and after hours of unexceptional trivia gathering, the Saturday edition of Great Falls Evening Tribune hit the streets, and no one seemed to be bothered by the lack of major news. "You know, we can't have a front page about floods and landslides with skeletons thrown about, not every week!" offered Aylrod.

"Thank God," added George Winslow as he walked out of the newsroom.

Anne Marie sighed, folded the newspaper, and tossed it into her handbag.

"You leaving early? Where's that motivation, that inspiration you had last week?" Several moments of silence followed. Aylrod cleared his throat. "Look," he said, "a week ago, I felt like taking you out for an early supper, and perhaps a glass of wine. I'm assuming you're over 21. But you looked so overwhelmed by the events of the day, I decided to postpone. Like today. What do you say, Anne Marie?"

She narrowed her eyes and pointed at him. "Aylrod…first of all, I *am* over 21. And I suppose a Saturday night out wouldn't hurt. But isn't there a bevy of beauties waiting for you somewhere?"

"You can be my beauty this evening. It would be an honor. I can pick you up at your apartment at 6 o'clock."

"Ok, it's a date. You know where I live?"

"Absolutely, I've been scouting out your place for months."

"Sure. So, where are we going? I want to dress appropriately."

Aylrod suggested The Ramshackle Inn, and Anne Marie agreed.

As they drove south on Riverside Road, they had to slow down as the repair crews had narrowed it down to one lane in the area of the landslide. At the old entrance to Mount Durham Cemetery, a policeman stopped the traffic to allow a series of trucks to head north.

"That's where Lou's Place was," Aylrod said to Anne Marie.

"What place? Oh, you mean the inn on the other side of the road?"

"Yep. They had to tear it down some time ago. It was quite a landmark, though. Known throughout the state. It's a good thing it wasn't there last week; the restaurant and hotel would have been victims of the landslide, just like the high cemetery ground."

"Lou's Place, Lou's Place." Anne Marie repeated the name. "I emember it from high school days when I would ride my bicycle down his way. And, when I was working at Graham's Department Store, the levator operator would talk about it all the time. He had worked there luring high school and the summer after graduation. John's his name and e's just a few years older than me. I had such a crush on him. He was ny first boyfriend."

"John, eh. And he was your first boyfriend. I should look him up. Ie might give me some hints on how to woo you."

"Don't worry, Aylrod. You don't need hints in the wooing lepartment."

They both laughed and just then the roadway cleared and on they vent to their Saturday night dinner date.

On the way back home a couple of hours later, Anne Marie asked f they could stop at the site of Lou's Place. It was totally dark despite a ull moon, but Aylrod turned into what had been the driveway to the stablishment. The two scanned the landscape but found no remnants of he tavern-restaurant-hotel.

"This was quite the hot spot for several years. People came from ar and wide for the food and the entertainment," Aylrod said.

Feeling the effects of her three glasses of wine that came with linner, Anne Marie offered coyly, "Well, we can create our own ntertainment, if you want."

Aylrod took the hint. The two started making out, kissing deeply, nd caressing otherwise forbidden parts in honor of the hot spot Lou's 'lace had been.

"So, how's the newspaper treating you?" asked John the elevato boy.

Anne Marie knew his daily routine and had stopped by at 2 p.m. a Graham's Department Store to join him for lunch. The thought came t her a few days after her Saturday night with Aylrod. She wondered if th goings-on at Lou's Place might have some connection to the discoverie of skeletons a mere 50 yards from the nightspot.

"It's treating me fine. I really like my work," she told John.

They bantered about between bites from their sandwiches and gulp from their sodas in the empty employee lunchroom. Finally, Anne Mari went for the target. "Have you been reading about the floods and th landslide at Mount Durham Cemetery? You know, my byline was on th breaking story when the police announced they had found a few skeleton at the site." She didn't give John a chance to reply. "That was on the hig ground facing the river. Lou's Place wasn't far from there. You worke at Lou's Place, didn't you?"

John hesitated. "I…did. Yes, I was a busboy after school, and worked in the kitchen the summer after graduation."

"Did you ever see anything suspicious? You know, the state polic forensic division has ruled the skeletons were not that old. I thought the might have been the bodies of slaves. You know there have been rumor all along about some of the farmers around there owning slaves in the 18 century. But the forensic report indicates the skeletons were all youn males who may have died 20 or so years ago. Did you ever see anythin that might indicate that's correct?"

John looked around the room. "Are you working on this? Are yo interviewing me?"

"Well, not yet. Probably never. I am simply doing background; am not quoting anyone."

"Anne Marie, anything I tell you has to be off the record."

"Don't worry. If there's something there, I'll find a way to protect
y sources. We don't have to do this here and now; we can meet more
iscretely at another time."

"Let me think about this."

"Ok. Let's keep in touch. You know how to reach me. But we
ouldn't wait too long. The story could get cold very fast. We should
lk again in a couple of days."

"Wow, Anne Marie, I hardly recognize you. What happened to the
niling young lady who kept the books and minded her business? What
as this newspaper work turned you into?"

Anne Marie let out a knowing smile. "A truth-seeker, or at least a
yline addict."

Exactly two days later, the duo met at the Great Falls Public Library
a corner of the reference room where they whispered for an hour. Once
gain, John required assurances that he would not be quoted, and Anne
arie agreed. She took out a brand-new notepad and placed several
encils in front of her, just in case.

What John revealed was that Lou's Place served as a rendezvous
te for men who sought out other men. They usually gathered in groups
f six or eight, they came from far and wide. They would eat and drink in
rivate dining rooms and occasionally they would be accompanied by
ome musicians and costumed singers. Nearly always, these men were
dults, but there were rare exceptions when one participant would bring
teenager with him. Occasionally, some would spend the night in the
otel rooms located at the back of the inn. There were also couples, most
f them adults of the same age, but often enough, the couple consisted of
n older man and a young man or a boy. It was suspected that the older
an was a priest. There was one fellow who made it known he was a
riest, loud and clear after a few drinks. He came from New Hampshire

and his last name started with Fitz, Fitzsomething. The staff called hi Friar Fritz. Another man suspected of being a priest always had two three youngsters with him, boys aged in their very early teens. He cam from up north, the mountain and lakes region and his underlings often h rosy cheeks. He referred to them as his 'cheery tomatoes.' Some of t men who came alone would try to entice some staffers to join them aft closing in one of the motel rooms. John swore he would never accept t invitation. But his co-workers, on occasion would, stating they did it f the payment they received. The summer after graduation, John wou help clean out rooms in the motel sections. Once in a while, there w evidence that there had been a fight the night before. Sometimes, one these priests who had come accompanied was seen driving away all alon John swore he was never involved with any goings-on.

Anne Marie gathered her notes and offered John the opportunity read them. He declined. She wished him well. As he left the room, Jo warned her that if she quoted him, he would deny everything.

Anne Marie reviewed her notes several times in the following day She didn't know what to do. Should she try to find someone who wou corroborate? Was this an angle worth pursuing? She realized finally th public interest in the landslide and the skeletons had waned. "It was aft all a cemetery. That's where you find dead people," she told herself. Sh wondered if she should share the information and the story idea it carri with Ed. Anne Marie decided she had already contributed to the 'Not to Print' file with her notes about the two boys killed at Tarawa. The was no need to hand over her notes about the priests and their young dat and have those notes become files in the 'morgue' at The Tribune. Sh realized that being a newspaper reporter was not being an investigato "Let someone else do the digging," she thought.

On the last day of April, a truly chilly day, Anne Marie found secluded spot in a vacant lot near her tenement building. She gathere some dead branches, lit a bonfire, and threw her notes about the custome of Lou's Place into the flames.

SIX

A CONSOLATION PRIZE

"Mrs. Wiggins. Are you done with today's paper?" Anne Marie asks, her upper body partly intruding into the nursing supervisor's office.

Mrs. Wiggins looks up from her desk, her face a perfect blend of surprise and annoyance. "Oh, the newspaper, yes…and no, I never had a chance to read it. The paper boy threw it in the middle of the driveway and the rain soaked it and it was useless. Like a bunch of wet rags."

"I was hoping to read about the storm, if there was any flooding."

"Well, Miss Dubois, you can watch the TV weather report later this afternoon."

"I know, but their weather is geared to the general area, all of New England, not the local scene. And, if there is any flooding, they would not even know about it until tomorrow. You see, Mrs. Wiggins, I am a newspaper junkie: get it fast, get it local." Anne Marie walks into the office and looks out the window behind Mrs. Wiggins' desk. "My, this storm means it. Reminds me of the flood of '44. Do you remember that one, with the landslides and everything?"

"Frankly, my dear, I don't. I vaguely remember my parents talking about it, but, goodness, that was over 60 years ago! I was a child."

"You know, Mrs. Wiggins, I was a reporter for the Tribune, and I covered the landslide at the Mount Durham Cemetery. That is the old colonial-era cemetery on Riverside Road. I was one of the first on the scene. I shared the byline of the article that ran on the front page that day. As a teenager, I explored that cemetery. Some historians claimed that the oldest part on the South side harbored the graves of slaves used in the early fields of the colony, but I never found any evidence of that..."

Mrs. Wiggins interrupts her and tersely says, "You can tell me all about it some other time. Right now, it's Friday morning and I've a ton of weekly reports to get ready for the Board of Directors."

Anne Marie retorts, "Well, have a good day, as we all drown here." She crosses the hallway into the lounge and, taking a seat facing the large windows, establishes herself as a weather observer might.

A few minutes later, Angie walks into the lounge and spots Anne Marie. "May I join you?" They both stare out the window for a while, examining the fine shrubbery to see if it survived the Maine winter. "I hate rainy days, especially in the early spring," she says.

"So do I," throws in Anne Marie. "The rain comes down with a vengeance. There are months of dirty snow and ice all over the place and now the rain is coming to wash it all away. That is what I would hear from these sheets of wind-driven torrent if they could speak. Everyone and everything becomes its victim. We are sheltered here, but the angry dampness assaults my every ache and weakness."

"That's so beautiful. What a great writer you must have been! And, you still are," whispers Angie. "But the rains seem to have stopped. In a few weeks, the sun and warmer temperatures will change the entire landscape."

Anne Marie turns to her and smiles. "You are correct, my dear. Thank you for your optimism. And, as soon as the weather permits, I am going to take you to see my old parish church, *Notre-Dame de la Consolation.* It is just two blocks from here."

"Oh, I can see the steeple from the window in my room. I've wondered about what church that is. *Notre-Dame*, you said...in French. Bravo! I can't wait to see it. I've always thought that the French-Canadian churches in New England were the most beautiful...very much like the ones throughout Québec. Ah...*Notre-Dame de la Consolation*, how appropriate!"

Betsy, the receptionist, walks into the lounge and announces: "There's a phone call for Miss Dubois..."

"What? I never get phone calls. Who is calling?" Anne Marie asks, a dose of irritation clearly visible on her voice.

"Male voice; says he's your nephew. He's on hold at the reception desk."

"Ok. Betsy, I will be right there," Anne Marie says in a low voice. Turning to Angie, she adds: "Somebody must have died."

"You have a nephew? I had no idea," Angie states.

"Yes, Oswald Dubois, my brother's only son. He lives in Florida. He is a sergeant, in charge of a U.S. Army recruiting station. My brother André, his father, escaped from Maine as soon as he could and moved to Miami decades ago. That is where Oswald, or Ozzie as we called him, was raised and that is where he returned after serving with the United States military intervention in Iraq."

"Well...hurry up and take the call. I'll be in my room," Angie offers as her blessing.

Anne Marie was grateful that Betsy had cleared the reception area.

"Ma tante? I'm so glad I've reached you; this is Sergeant Dubois your nephew."

"Yes. Good to hear from you, Ozzie."

"So, ma tante, I just wanted to know how you're doing. Still at the nursing home, I assume. How are they treating you? I plan on being up your way sometime soon and I hope I can stop to see you."

Betsy walks into the room and starts organizing the collection o items on her desk. "Please keep it brief," she whispers to Anne Marie.

"My mother has been in the hospital here in Florida." Ozzie offers

"I hope she gets well, and they let her go home."

"I doubt she will be going to her condo, more likely a nursing home I hope she adjusts well. I know it can be difficult." Betsy's activity wa constantly distracting Anne Marie and after a minute or two, she says t Ozzie, "Look, my dear, this is not a good time. I am so glad you called and I look forward to your visit when we can chat to our hearts' content."

"Good. I'm so glad we can get together. I have so many question about Canada. I'm thinking of buying the family farm at Saint Caesar," Ozzie says without realizing that his aunt had already hung up.

With the return of the warm spring sunshine, the nursing hom residents were now able to wander outside.

"Didn't you say it was just down the street? I'm totally out o breath. And, when you said we could go for a walk, I didn't know yo meant an expedition. This is an expedition. And, by the way, I'm sure w are in violation of some rule of the Washburn Home."

Anne Marie replies, "Let me take those one at a time. I did not sa 'just down the street,' I said the church was two blocks from the nursin ome. It is all downhill...an easy walk. And today is such a beautiful day, perfect day for a short walk."

"Downhill, right. But going back will be uphill," Angie retorts.

"Cannot argue with you there, what goes downhill goes uphill in e opposite direction. That is very basic. And to answer your second oint, yes, we are in violation of the rules. We should not leave the Vashburn Home without permission. But I have gone out many times by yself and nobody missed me. And, if they did, they would send Tom ut to fetch me, and if that happens today, Tom will find us at my usual estination, and we will have a ride back to the nursing home."

"My, my, Anne Marie, you think of everything, you've got an nswer for everything."

"There it is, that is my church, *Notre-Dame de la Consolation*. You e the steeple? Just a few more steps. We will take them slowly. Look, ere is a lovely bench halfway to the entrance. We can rest there and tch our breath."

A few moments later, Anne Marie bursts out with, "What is the atter with you anyway? You are never out of breath. I am the older one, e one who should be gasping and panting."

"Frankly, I don't know. When I woke up this morning, I had a oughing spell. And it came back after lunch. I don't know what's going n."

"Well, we can pray it will go away," Anne Marie says.

Suddenly, Angie yells out. "But the church is closed. Look at the O TRESPASSING sign."

"Oh, did I not tell you?"

"No. You did not. Why would we come here? We can't even go side. Anne Marie, did you know it was closed?"

"Yes, I did. When I returned to the nursing home after my last cursion here, and after Mrs. Wiggins had lashed out with the usual

scolding, she told me the church had been closed for almost a yea
'Didn't you see the No Trespassing sign?' she asked. I told her I did n
see the sign, and she replied that 'some people only see what they wa
to see.' Do not worry, my dear. There is a bench right there. We can ha
a seat and rest, the sun is nice and warm, and we can admire t
architecture and we can even meditate and pray, if you want."

"I do pray. But meditate? Not since leaving the convent. An
Marie, what are you thinking?"

"We could, I guess, simply talk about religious things. Since y
told me about your convent life, I have wondered about it. I was never
religious person, *au contraire*, and I have often wondered how a pers
could lead such a life, and for so long, and how you have been since y
left."

"Did we have to come here to talk about all that?"

Eventually, the two ladies sit down on the bench, and they eleva
their gaze to the arched window above the principal door. "Obviously, v
are on the wrong side. To see it clearly, one should be inside the churc
The sunlight hits the stained glass and illuminates the scene. I rememb
the window portraying the baptism of Christ by John the Baptist. It
lovely. The story goes that the priest who founded the parish, back in t
1870s, wanted to name it after Saint John the Baptist, *Saint-Jean Baptis*
to be precise, the patron saint of French Canada. But the Irish bish
refused to approve the name. He said there were too many churches
that name. Whenever a French-Canadian community in Maine reach
the level of having its own parish, they always wanted it named aft
Saint-Jean Baptiste. The bishop compromised, however, and gave t
church the name of *Notre-Dame*. The pastor resisted countering th
every town with an Irish congregation had a Saint Patrick church. F
insisted, however, on adding the term 'consolation,' making sure t
parish would be known as *Notre-Dame de la Consolation.* I suppose l
saw it as a sort of consolation prize. But the stained-glass window w
already on order, and it was installed."

"You certainly know your history, Anne Marie."

"I did quite a bit of research for an article at the time of the centennial of the parish. The newspaper ran the article on Page One with a photograph of the name above the lintel that you see up there. This is where I was baptized and where I had my first communion. Oh, my *Maman* was so proud that day. She was a devoted member of *Les Dames de Sainte-Anne*, working every Bingo night for the organization. Of course, you know that in order to receive your first communion, you have to make your first confession. The priest had rehearsed the entire class on the formula and the kinds of sins that one confesses. 'Bless me, Father, for I have sinned…' The formula goes on to say, 'It has been one week, one month, six months, whatever, since my last confession.' But obviously, that does not hold for the first time. And I just picked a sin from the list provided. I remember saying I had lied ten times, and the priest on the other side of the confessional screen looked at me in disbelief."

Angie gives a brief chuckle.

The two ladies fall into a pensive silence. They watch the sun's rays lose their strength, and they feel the temperature dip.

"Well, Angie, we should get you back to the nursing home, before you catch pneumonia," the older woman says with a chuckle.

"I'm ok. We can stay a bit longer."

After another moment of silence not without a dash of awkwardness, Anne Marie resumes the conversation, focusing on Angie's years in the convent.

Angie hesitates. "You know, I've never talked about this. Well, that's not exact. We all had a spiritual advisor, a confessor of sorts, whom we would meet on a regular basis. And those sessions often brought up some issues. But, in retrospect, they were minor issues. Our lives were managed very carefully. We had our work – teaching in my case – and a routine of housekeeping chores, plus a full slate of religious observances, you know, daily mass, benediction just before supper, hours of adoration on special feasts. It was all organized for us – pre-ordained. All we had to do was follow. I rarely had time to question anything. It was all formula and ritual, used and tested for centuries. Who was I to question anything?"

"How do you deal with being a layperson now, here at the nursing home?"

"I still have the ritual and formula within me. I spent a lifetime with that. It's integrated, part of me. I know nothing else. And, besides, I'm not like you, Anne Marie. You've spent a lifetime questioning, looking, searching. In my life, there was room for only one byline, and it wasn't mine. It was God and centuries of religious superiors who wrote the daily journal, if you get what I mean. And let's be practical. What else am I going to do? I'm old and being cared for. What am I going to do? Go out and join the *Folies Bergères*?"

Anne Marie giggles. "Well, if you did, I would be your biggest fan."

A heavy cloud passes over the late afternoon sun and the two ladies find themselves in a darkened space. Several moments of silence also fill the space. Angie reads the memorial plaque attached to the back of the bench. "This name here, the last one, Reverend Laroche...did you know him?"

"Oh, yes, I did. That is a long story. He was my confessor. Not when I made my first communion. Much later, when I was working at the newspaper. He died in 1972...I haven't been to confession since."

The conversation halts as a van pulls up in front of *Notre-Dame*. Anne Marie recognizes it immediately, while Angie casts a puzzled glare.

"I knew I'd find you here. Now, get in the van," Tom says, opening the door. "Time to go home."

SEVEN

MEANWHILE, IN THE SUNSHINE STATE

She emerged from her medical haze and saw that she wasn't alone. "Well! It's about time," the old woman said. She clicked off the TV set and turned to confront her visitor. "Thought you had abandoned me."

"Never, Mother, would I abandon you," Sarge replied in a nonotone. He sighed the sigh of a prodigal son as he dropped his body ıeavily into the visitor's chair.

"Well, I feel abandoned. Nobody ever visits, not even the ladies vhere I used to live, you know, my so-called best friends. And you, my only son, you're all I have left, and I hardly ever see you.

Sarge wanted to turn the TV back on. Instead, he examined the old voman with unkempt hair and gray skin, wrapped in a wrinkled cotton heet. He went to her and propped her up, silently reading her name on a lip of paper attached to the bed: Sandra L. Johnson. "I know I've asked ou this before. When you married my father years ago, why didn't you ake his name, Dubois? Why did you insist on keeping the Johnson name?

Her eyes grew larger. "Yes, Ozzie you've asked me that before an I told you before. I just did not want to be taken for one of those creep Canadian tourists pouring into Florida."

Sarge wanted to scream and run out of the room. He stood silentl in the doorway and searched the hallway for help. Moments later, he saic "So, dear mother, how are you feeling?"

"How should I know? They don't tell me anything. They just smile bring me pills, and give me injections. Even if they talked to me, probably wouldn't understand. The place is crawling with foreigners."

"Ok, mother dear, enough of that. This is a perfectly fine hospital. Sarge knew it wasn't the best facility, but it was what her insuranc company covered. He shared his mother's distrust of the entire medica establishment in South Florida, but he wasn't going to share hi misgivings with her. "I'm sure you're getting the best possible care," h said firmly. "And, when it's time, you'll be released and sent to som rehab facility."

"Why don't they just kill me right now and have it done with?"

"Mother, don't talk like that, please!"

A young hospital worker pushed the door open and cheerily greete Mrs. Johnson. "How are we doing this evening?" She didn't expect a answer. The nursing assistant took a small paper cup like the kind you pu ketchup in at a fast-food restaurant and placed it on the patient's tray "Now, these are your pills for tonight...so we can have a good night' sleep. She patted down the spread at the foot of the bed, sent identica smiles, first to the patient and then to her visitor, and walked out of th room.

Mrs. Johnson made a face, sticking out her tongue in the directio of the corridor. "It's always *we*. We do this, we do that. I have nothing t do with that person. There's no *we* here."

Sarge didn't respond. There was nothing to be said; he just wante to leave.

His mother ignored the hesitation. "I just hope they don't keep me anging on like they did with your poor father. Heavens, all those tubes ad wires and more pills...I hope they don't stretch it out for me. Your oor, poor father. Oh, it was so sad, and it took so long. Promise me, zzie, you won't let them turn me into a vegetable like they did to your oor father."

"Don't worry, we won't let you become a vegetable." As he used e word *we*, Sarge entertained a mischievous laugh deep inside. He oked at his mother and wondered what kind of vegetable she could ecome: something sour and ugly, a prune, no that's some fruit, more kely a turnip, an onion, a horseradish, something like that.

"I just hope you're around to make sure," she said. "I know you ever came around when your father was dying. Too busy, I suppose."

"Mother!" Sarge screamed. "Mother, I was in Iraq. You damn well now that I was in Iraq. You damn well know I would have been here, by s side, if I could have. Oh, mother, you're such a vicious old lady." arge examined his mother; he stared at her intently. He turned away and alked out of the room, down the hallway, and into the darkened parking t of Southgate Memorial Hospital.

On his way home, Sergeant Dubois stopped at his favorite haunt: ucky's Bar and Grill in Fort Lauderdale.

"Hey." With just one word, he greeted the guy, a twenty-something llow with a shaved head and a goatee who was occupying what Sarge onsidered his usual bar stool.

"Hey," the man replied, not even looking up from his frosty beer ug.

Sarge stood silently behind him, waiting for some further wo from the new guy. Sarge threw a glance at the vacant seats on each sid "How's it going?" Sarge asked.

"Ok. Eh, just fine, I guess," said the guy with the mug, stretchi each word's musicality, like a baritone saxophone. Never turning, lowered his head and allowed his mouth to meet the beer mug, his arn folded to support his chin, his lips in repose on the rim of the glass. Sar decided to let the man be and he slipped himself onto the bar stool ne to him. Stirred, the guy bolted upright, frosty brew dripping from h bottom lip. "Hey," he said in a low voice. "Mind if I sit here?" Sar didn't expect an answer, yet he hoped the question would penetrate h neighbor's fogginess, that he'd get up, that he'd offer his seat to Sarg "Go ahead. It's a free country." The man still spoke slowly, as if it was chore.

As he settled himself in, Sgt. Smith surveyed the Saturday nig crowd. He found a few familiar faces; no one he really knew, certain nobody he wanted to spend the evening joking and laughing with. T room was loud, people trying to outdo each other, trying to drown out t DJ sound. A jovial group, slap-friendly, eager, horny even.

"Guess you're back to your old habits: your Saturday night routin I mean," offered Chuck the bartender.

"Guess so. And how's it going, Chuck? Looks busy."

"That it is. Loud, fussy, and bad tippers. Unlike you, Sergea Smith. Can I get you your usual?"

"Yup. Old habits never die!"

A few minutes later, a foursome of young women all prettied up f their night out rushed up to the bar and swamped Chuck with a chorus drink orders. They spoke all at once in high-pitched squeals a performed a little dance around the last empty barstool. Sarge w annoyed; he joined his neighbor with the goatee in a slumping retre The girls spotted a group of friends across the room, and they rush towards them, yelling and screaming.

"Stupid sorority girls," said Chuck as he counted the quarters they left as their tip.

"Redundant," muttered the guy with the goatee.

"What?" asked Chuck.

"Stupid, sorority, girls. Three words that mean the same. That's what I mean," replied the goateed fellow. He spoke slowly, the words finding their proper sequence with evident difficulty.

"Yeah. Makes sense." Sarge tried to hide his amazement. Not only could this kid say more than two words at a time, but he also sounded quite lucid. "You seem to be an intelligent young man," Sarge said.

"I see you two are on speaking terms," the bartender said.

"Not really," said the younger man. He dropped his shaved head back in the cradle of his folded arms. Sarge gave Chuck a quizzical look, and the bartender inched his face close and whispered that the kid had been there since 3 o'clock in the afternoon. "I cut him off after his last beer, that one that he's sleeping with." Chuck laughed as he rushed off to fill someone's drink order at the far end of the bar.

Sarge swiveled his body to face the Saturday night crowd. He leaned backward and enjoyed the pressure of the counter on his lower back. He allowed the stiffness in his muscles to ease. He scanned the room and took on the role of spectator.

"Hey, kid." Chuck was back. "Hey, you ok?" There was no answer from the guy with the beer mug. Chuck nudged him on the shoulder. Sarge watched and then joined in. "Wake up, young man," he said as he sent a puzzled glance towards the bartender. Sarge started to rise from his seat. The sliding movement began very slowly, almost imperceptibly. The young man's body swayed away from the counter and dropped limply into Sarge's lap. Sarge sat back with a thud, the heavy body of his neighbor pinning him there. He grabbed the kid's head and stared at his face. "Call 911," he yelled to Chuck. "Call 911. Now! Some of the bar patrons pulled back, creating an open space in front of Sarge and his inanimate neighbor. Everyone turned to stare. The music stopped. Overdose, passed out, and heart attack were among the diagnostics bandied around the room. Chuck attempted to calm everyone down. "No need to panic. It's under control," he said. Nobody was convinced and within minutes the place was empty.

"Let me help you," Chuck said. "He'll be better on the floor." Sergeant Smith didn't hear him. The sound of explosions enveloped him. Gunfire filled his ears. He was sitting in the middle of a dusty desert road in Iraq and his buddy was in his arms. Like a pieta, Sarge held his fellow soldier, in the same way he was now holding this stranger in Lucky's Bar. The face of death on the soldier years before and the one Sarge now contemplated were identical.

EIGHT

THE MORGUE AND A CAN OF WORMS

"We still have a date tonight, don't we?" Aylrod whispered. "I can make a reservation for dinner at the Whitney Hotel next door. At what time?" He waited a few minutes for Ann Marie to answer. It was late in the afternoon, the day's edition of the Tribune had been put to rest for a couple of hours, and everyone – nearly everyone had gone home. Time for supper. Aylrod and Anne Marie were in the doorway of the newsroom, whispering soft sweet things to each other.

"Let's go up to the morgue and talk about it," Anne Marie said.

"What's to talk about?"

"Well...I don't know if we have a good thing going. I've told you...I'm not sure I can do this, you know, having an affair. If we have sex again, it will be our seventh time..."

"Oh, somebody's counting!"

"Let's go upstairs and talk about it. Please, Aylrod."

"Ok, after you, young lady," Aylrod said with a graceful bow, hi hand pointing to the staircase. They were halfway up when Laura, th switchboard operator, came out of the ladies' room and starte straightening out the area for the evening shift. She stretched her nec around the stairs to see who was there. "Humph...trouble in th trousers...and his latest prey," she mumbled.

The "morgue" is small and crowded with large binders on the fe desks, and several file drawers surrounding them. The lights are feebl and bent here and there where the readers have left them following the research. Anne Marie looked out the window at the Public Library acros the street and the fancy hotel next door where Aylrod liked to hang ou A fine layer of dust covers everything.

Within seconds, Aylrod had his pants down and was pulling a Anne Marie's blouse. He started kissing her and she responded. Ann Marie knew that the sweat of their encounter was all that would remair Everything else would evaporate. The pain, the excitement, the dread, th pleasure, they would find that place in her mind where not even vagu recollections survived. Her feelings would be obliterated, smashed int nothingness. But, the sweat, not only the odors...his and hers...and th silky chalkiness of the dust would make its way into every fold of he body. Anne Marie knew that's what her brain would not be able t eradicate. Yet, she didn't stop him. She placed her hands firmly on hi back and held him tightly against her torso. She told herself that her hand should remain neutral, yet moments later, she placed them on his hip where they merged with the movements of his lower body. She quickl retracted them, lifting them up and holding them over her head, wavin them rhythmically in the air until they fell back to his shoulders. Thei lips connected. He pushed her high against the wall. His movement accelerated. He started yelling "Oh, yes! Oh, yes. Oh yes. Yes, yes."

He drew his lips from hers and dropped his forehead to he shoulder. She felt his wet hair brush her neck. He pulled away and sa the drawer with the file name "Unfit to print" and whispered, "that wa definitely fit to print."

She pushed his body away from her and held him at arm's length.)epends on who's writing it," she replied. They stood in the middle of e room and rearranged their clothing.

The couple emerged from the morgue and silently descended to the ain entrance. On the sidewalk, she took several steps away from him. ıe looked around, and seeing no one, she coughed. She cleared her roat and coughed a few more times. She stood in the shadow of the ewspaper building, and spit repeatedly, sending her phlegm to splatter gainst the cornerstone of the structure. Aylrod headed toward the nployee parking lot; Anne Marie started walking toward the tenements. ıe used her hands to organize her hair, to press her bodice in place, to ften the pleats of her skirt, all the while, brushing off the chalky dust of e morgue.

A few steps later, she felt the liquid between her legs. She stopped ıd squeezed her thighs. She looked about and seeing nobody, she ached under her skirt and pulled her panties off. She nearly lost her ılance as she extracted the wet undergarment. Finally, she held her ınties in her hand, rolled into a tight ball. Anne Marie walked to the reet corner and dropped the offending garment into the mailbox.

She couldn't sleep and she got up much earlier than usual. Anne arie's latest nightmare had been terrifying. She kept hearing the baby's reams from the mailbox outside the newspaper office. "Mommy, get e out of here," the child would say again and again, often adding the me request to her daddy. "I know you're in there, daddy. Come and scue me, please, please." Her solution was to get out of bed while it was ill dark and get dressed. She looked in her mother's room and was tisfied to find her still asleep.

One hour later, Anne Marie stood out in front of Nichol's Tea oom, waiting along with a half-dozen early risers for the restaurant to pen. Suddenly, she felt someone nudging her and when she looked up, she recognized Laura. "Wow, I've never seen you so early, Anne Marie the switchboard operator said teasingly. The newspaper reporter didr know what to say except "Good morning, Laura." At that moment, tl doors opened, and the early breakfast group started walking in. An Marie realized that she and Laura had had few moments to chat and to g to know each other in the four years since she had started working at tl Great Falls Evening Tribune. "May I join you for breakfast?" Anne Mar asked. Laura nodded and smiled.

Halfway through their meal out of the blue, Laura said "You kno I saw the two of you yesterday as you climbed the stairs and went into tl morgue. "Oh, you did," Anne Marie said, adding, "Oh...we had to che some archives..." Laura laughed and said "Archives...that's what you c having sex." A powerful silence followed. Anne Marie wanted to get and run, but she sipped her coffee and played with her utensils. "Lo dear, it's none of my business, but if you're interested, there's a lot I c tell you about dear, dear Aylrod."

Laura had quite a tale to share. She and Aylrod started dati sometime before but had split up by the time Anne Marie showed up the newsroom. Often, Aylrod rented one of the cheap rooms at the Reg Lounge and they spent the night there. Laura became pregnant a suffered a miscarriage. She got pregnant a second time and she decid to have an abortion. She knew it was illegal, but her cousin Lucy told h that she knew of an abortion clinic being operated by a physician in small town up-country, where the local agricultural lodge had closed a it was being used as an unofficial hospital for dozens of young girls. neighbor of hers became aware of the situation. She was Catholic and to Laura of a nun-operated home for unwed mothers located in a bord town on the Maine-New Hampshire state line. She highly recommend it based on her own experience more than twenty years before and to Laura that her baby born in that setting would eventually go into Catholic orphanage in Great Falls and later to a seminary to study for tl priesthood. Laura wasn't interested in spending all those months aw from work so she could have a baby that would be considered fodder f the priesthood. A few weeks after the abortion, Aylrod found a new obje for his affection, a new teacher at the local junior high school, but that did not last long. "And then, my dear Anne Marie, you came along."

Two days later, anticipating what she called the 'epitome of routine,' Anne Marie headed to the police station. The police station was located at the rear of City Hall which was closed on Saturdays as was the District Court. She scanned the police blotter with its usual list of traffic problems and possible arrests from the customary Friday night barroom fights that filled up the local news section she was responsible for. There was no reason to expect anything else on that unusually mild morning in late February.

As she entered, she was surprised to see the police chief present along with two men in civilian clothing seated in his office. When Chief Callahan saw Anne Marie, he closed the door. "Wow, what's he doing here on a Saturday morning?" she whispered to herself. The news reporter went to her usual spot and looked for the police logbook only to discover it was missing.

"Where's the blotter?" she asked the sergeant who was manning the desk.

"The chief's got it," was the reply.

"Oh. I did notice that Chief Callahan is in this morning. On a Saturday, that's quite unusual," Anne Marie said. "And, who's that with him in his office?"

"I'm not at liberty to comment," the sergeant said.

Anne Marie stepped outside and posted herself at the side entrance. In the cooler air of late winter, she pondered. She whispered to herself. "Maybe the routine has lost its epitome."

Half an hour later, Ed, the editor, joined her. “What’s going on?” he said. “Chief Callahan called me and said I should come over. Is he here? What’s happening?”

“I have no idea. He rarely comes in on a Saturday. I saw him in his office. He has two visitors,” Anne Marie replied.

Just then, the chief pocked his head outside. “Come in. We have a very difficult situation. I’ve prepared a press release.” He had Ed and Anne Marie escorted to his office, invited them to sit down, and handed a piece of paper to Ed. “I’m sorry, but I only have one copy.”

While Ed was reading the short type-written text, the chief told Anne Marie that the two men she had seen in his office were from Augusta. One of them represented the Capitol Police and the other was from the Vice Squad of the State Police. When he was finished, Ed handed the text to Anne Marie. Then he took it back.

“I’ll read it for you. This is very troubling.”

- A triple fatality was discovered at 1:30 a.m. today on Lake View Road. It appears that two vehicles were involved. There was major damage to the vehicles and in the wreckage, three bodies were found.

- The victims are State Senator Robert Pothier of Great Falls age 72; Daniel Stackhouse also of Great Falls, age 17; an unidentified woman, address unknown, apparently in her 30s.

- Evidence points to a full head-on collision at the bottom of a steep hill.

Silence followed the reading. The chief stated that the investigation is ongoing, adding that the text Ed has just read is the only official statement at this time. “You may print this in today’s edition. The news staff can conduct its own investigation and print any additional information you deem pertinent. If we have anything to add, we’ll let you

:now. It is 10 o'clock now and I know you go to press at 2 p.m. I doubt ve will have anything new. This is going to take time. There are many uestions."

As they walked back to the newspaper office, Ed said they would repare a page-one notice with the text just handed to them. "Senator 'othier is well known statewide. He's been in politics for decades. I'm ure we have some bio information in the morgue, including a photo. I'm ssigning you, Anne Marie, to come up with an obituary for today's dition. Call his office and find out which funeral home has his remains. 'ind out what you can about funeral services."

"Yes sir," she said, saluting him like a good recruit. "The obituary irl reporting for duty."

NINE

THE ANGRY RECRUITER

The parking space in front of the recruiting station, *his* parking space, was occupied by a souped-up pickup truck with Colorado license plates and a gold-tasseled Puerto Rican flag hanging from the rear-view mirror. Sarge remembered that a new associate cruiter was starting today.

"Gonna have to teach your new boy where to park," said one of the ilors in his spotless whites nursing a cigarette on the sidewalk.

"Guess so," Sgt. Dubois replied. He had no use for the Navy cruiters. Or the Air Force guys. Prissy and snobby, he considered them. ie only real soldiers were the Army guys and maybe the Marines. The rvices occupied nearly an entire wing of the shopping plaza and had come the largest Armed Services Recruiting Station in South Florida. ust because we work together doesn't mean we have to like each other' d become Sgt. Dubois' motto in recent months. It seemed the ighboring recruiters were younger and more competitive, sometimes costing his Army candidates outside and giving them a sales talk about eir own branch of the services. And most of them were smokers. lways on the sidewalks flirting with the girls on their way to the check-cashing store or the nail salon. All of which was strictly forbidden for t men who worked in Sarge's office.

The new recruiter he requested was Spanish-speaking, and Sar thought better than starting their work relationship with a lecture where not to park. He needed all the help he could get in attracting t growing number of Hispanic kids in area high schools.

"Sir!" The young recruiter snapped to attention. "Sergeant Man Esperanza reporting, sir."

"No need to salute here, Sergeant Esperanza." Sarge closed the do and extended his hand invitingly. "We're in the civilian world he We're still in the military, but we live and work in a civilian environme Your military outfit is required, however. It's a selling point. And we' on a first-name basis, Manny. Except that I don't have one. I'm just Sarg Plain old Sarge. And forget the old part. And, by the way, don't park the anymore. That's my space," Sarge said, pointing out the office windo to the parking lot. "You don't have to move that fancy truck. Ju remember tomorrow morning. Now, let me introduce you to the rest the crew, as I show you around the office."

They were stunning. Simply beautiful boys. Sarge stood at his de and greeted them. They offered him a polite handshake and smiled the identical smiles. The recruiter fell into a haze of subtle admiration: t pinkish brown of youthful skin, the depth of their near-black eye generous locks of hair framing high intelligent brows. Sarge question his reaction, judging it to be homoerotic and distasteful. He shook h head nervously while convincing himself that the boys' beauty had feminine quality. That made him feel safer.

"The Guerrero brothers," Sgt. Esperanza said with a touch triumph as he escorted them into the recruiting station.

"Glad to meet you," offered Sgt. Dubois. Slender and tall, the boys towered over his desk. "Sit down," he said, and he pulled over a second chair. "Let's talk about your career with the United States Army." Sarge had already reviewed their dossiers. On paper, the recruits were ideal candidates. Their scores were up there, they were physically fit, and they seemed eager.

Sgt. Manny Esperanza hadn't wasted any time since his arrival two months earlier. Within a couple of weeks, he had mapped out a strategy that focused on high schools in Hispanic communities; he had identified principals and guidance counselors and with his lists, he started his rounds. Sgt. Dubois was glad to have him second in command and gave him pretty much carte blanche. Sgt. Esperanza's enthusiasm started bearing fruit quickly and among his first potential enlistees were Roberto and Federico Guerrero. Sons of Cuban immigrants, the 19-year-old twin brothers had graduated with honors from Lauderdale Pines High School but had floundered for nearly a year unable to get into college and find a permanent job. Sarge recited his welcoming pep talk and the boys nodded in near unison, throwing their "yes sirs" at the appropriate times in soft respectful Spanish-accented tones. Manny, their sponsor, stood behind them, beaming like a guardian angel.

The scene was popping with energy. The commuter van from the airport hummed and vibrated like a racehorse waiting for the flag to drop. The seven recruits who made up this class seemed anxious and acted as if they could taste the upcoming adventure. The driver nervously checked his watch. He stared at Sarge standing on the sidewalk in front of the recruiting office.

Sargeant Dubois was reading from a new script. He was elsewhere; a new place, a new time. His eyes were scanning casualty lists and he recognized two names. He heard the television newsmen waiting around the corner, he heard the parents' wails, and he saw the flags neatly folded, two identical flags.

"Don't worry, Sarge, they'll make it all right." Sgt. Esperanza placed his hand on his superior officer's back. "This is a good batch of kids. They'll make it through basic training with flying colors."

The driver opened his window and asked: "Can we leave now?"

Sarge waved him on. He felt the sweat dribble down his back. He forced himself to remain standing, as if at attention, and stare directly at the commuter van as it lurched forward.

The Guerrero brothers peered out of the side window, opened it, and smiled their angelic farewell. "Innocence. Beautiful innocence," Sarge said out loud as he watched the vehicle fade away.

He stood still scanning the roofline for snipers, examining the parking lot, sure that some of the vehicles were booby-trapped. He closed his eyes; he shook his head violently. "No, no," he yelled out. "You're not here. Dammit, get out of my head," he said, searching for the words of the exorcist. "This is not the same place...not the same time. Leave me alone."

On the bottom edge of a sleepless night, Sarge drove to work and buried himself in minutiae. Before any other recruiters arrived, he swept the floor and tidied up. He was about to put away the files on the class of recruits that had flown to basic training in Georgia the day before. Their photographs took on new lives. He focused on the Guerrero twins. As far as he knew, nobody had ever recruited brothers, certainly not identical twins. Sarge shoved the folders into the file cabinet. He didn't want to see their faces. He closed his eyes tightly and dropped into his chair. He massaged his brow and gradually the golden sands of desert roads in Iraq appeared before him, and so did the anonymous streets of insurgent towns. One by one, the faces of dead soldiers paraded before him.

"Sgt. Esperanza, come here," he said as the new recruiter entered ıe office. "Look, it's too late now, but I don't think it's a good idea to ecruit two brothers and send them to war. Not at the same time. Not now, ot this war."

"You talking about the Guerreros? What's wrong with them, sir?

"Nothing, and that's part of the problem," Sarge answered in a tone o somber it seemed to reach beyond the walls of the office. "Manny, ou're aware of the high casualty rates. Could you face the parents if both ons were killed in battle?"

"Sir, no one wants to face the parents of dead soldiers. Sir, these oys are fighters. Look at their name: Guerrero means warrior. They're ough, they'll survive."

"Manny, I've seen lots of tough soldiers who didn't survive."

The room was quiet. The young recruiter searched for words. autiously, he ventured, "Sir, with all due respect...if we had to think bout soldiers who don't survive, we'd recruit no one." Sgt. Esperanza aluted and left the room.

The news from Iraq was not allowed to penetrate the wall of fficiency and determination that Sergeant Oswald Dubois had onstructed at the Banyan Cove U.S. Army Recruiting Station. If the ıembers of his staff were aware of what was going on in Iraq, they knew etter than to talk about it. They focused on their mission: meet the uotas, fill out the paperwork, stay in shape, look sharp, and set an xample. Sgt. Dubois didn't permit himself to share his ambivalence. here was good news: the decrease in violence since the surge of the past pring. And, there was still plenty of bad news: more than 3,000 merican soldiers dead and still dying; army ranks stretched to the limit; onstant leaks about falsified documents and wasted money. Sgt. Dubois vasn't surprised that the army had sent previously injured soldiers back to Iraq and that the Pentagon had omitted hundreds of soldiers from th wounded lists. He had lost all confidence and trust. He kept looking i the mirror searching for the gung-ho recruit of previous days, and h wasn't there. Instead, Oswald saw a bitter, angry bureaucrat whose jo was to sell something he knew didn't work.

His home-based internet scouring had linked him to a few anti-wa websites, and he had connected with Iraq veterans opposed to the war a well as a fringe group urging members of the military to go AWOL.

Sergeant Manny Esperanza was torn between friendship with hi boss and his loyalty to duty. Every day, Sarge seemed more depressed. I the past few weeks, Manny had seen his boss drive into the parking lo only to sit in his car for several minutes and suddenly drive away.

On a Tuesday morning, moments after opening the office, Sg Esperanza answered a phone call meant for Sarge who as usual was late Manny listened carefully and knew immediately the news woul devastate the boss. "This is going to send him over the edge," he said t himself immediately upon hanging up. He decided to leave a writte report, maybe to soften the blow. He scanned the parking lot and wa relieved to see that Sarge's parking space was empty. Manny starte producing his summary of the phone conversation.

> "The chaplain at Fort Benning in Georgia reported that Pvt. Federico Guerrero had been involved in a motor vehicle accident over the weekend. The accident occurred off base early Sunday morning and involved an Army jeep that plunged into a lagoon. The body of Pvt. Guerrero of Lauderdale Pines, Florida, was retrieved from the water later in the day and he was declared dead at the scene. It appears there was no one else involved in the accident.

There was no evidence of liquor or drugs. The recruiting staff in Banyan Cove, Florida, is requested to inform the family in the first instance, following the standard protocol. The press release will be issued only after next of kin notification."

Sgt. Esperanza reread the report, signed it, and placed it ategically in the center of Sgt. Dubois' desk. He remembered the nversation the day the Guerrero twins took off for camp; something had unched a premonition and Sarge seemed to know that the boys would eet a bad fate. He had yelled out his question: "Could you face the rents and tell them that their sons had died?" The memory made him k, and he dashed to the bathroom. The sour smells of his breakfast still inging to him, Manny emerged several minutes later to find Sgt. Dubois nding at his desk reading the note about the accident at boot camp.

"Jesus Christ. Jesus Fuckin Christ," Sarge said under his breath. ith his free hand, he wiped the sweat off his forehead, his swears appearing on his lips again and again, each time more menacingly. The o men stared at each other. They stood motionless. The older man's ce turned a shade of gray. "Christ, we don't even have to send them to q to get them killed," he said.

"Sir," said the younger man. He scraped his brain looking for a rther response but came up with emptiness. "Sir."

"Save it, Sergeant. Save it for Mister and Missus Guerrero."

"Me?"

"Yes. You! I'm out of here."

Manny followed his boss outside and in doing so almost knocked er two Asian women on their way to the nail salon next door. ergeant Dubois, Sarge what am I supposed to do?"

"Look it up in the manuals. Call up someone at headquarters. andle it, Sergeant."

"But..."

"Listen, Manny. This is yours. Just take care of it. I'm out of re."

TEN

FINAL DRAFTS

She spoke softly. "It was quite a while ago, but some days it feels like yesterday...and since it was way before I met you, my dear canaries, I would love to share that memory with you." Anne Marie decides to spend the afternoon in her special space. She wants to bask in the tranquility of her closet. "Oh, dear Father, Son, and you too, Holy Ghost, it has been so hectic these days. I am so grateful that Angie is here, but she talks so much. I guess it is all that time spent in silence during her convent years. Now she feels she must fill that void. And, my dear birds, I will be having some company. My nephew just telephoned me this noon to say he is on his way and that he can't wait to see me after all those years. Ozzie, that's his name, expects to be here tomorrow evening. He hinted that he will have some important news."

If the canaries could talk back to her, they might ask her about the memory she promised to share with them.

Anne Marie pushes apart the curtain surrounding the closet and removes her sweater. "My, my, my, it gets so hot in here. Of course, it's June...almost summer. Anyway, I was about to tell you about my last day at the Tribune. That was in 1993; I had just turned 72."

She then starts to narrate her story:

I was sitting in the upstairs office when I heard a gentle knock on the frame of the open door. I said, "Oh, Donald, come in. Did you find one?"

"Yes, madam, a Phillips screwdriver. Is it okay if I unscrew the sign now? If you prefer, I can come back later."

"No please, just go ahead. I am just gathering my things."

I watched Donald, the janitor, attack the small sign on the office door. The metal sign had etched itself into the wood panel and seemed reluctant to give in to the twisting of the screwdriver.

I resisted the urge to take a couple of photos – before and after shots: the first picture of the heavy door with the sign in the middle of the upper part, announcing *Miss Anne Marie Dubois* on one line and just below it, *Executive Editor*, and the second photo of the empty door showing the original hues of the varnish and the space the sign had occupied for the past eleven years.

"There, got it. Do you want to keep the sign, Miss Dubois? To keep as a souvenir?"

"Well, I hadn't thought of it, but I suppose it belongs with all this other stuff I am taking with me. I doubt if there will ever be another executive editor with that name at the Tribune. Yes, put it right here on the desk and I will pack it with all my things." I watched Donald wipe the sign in a useless attempt to polish it and then deposit it on the desk, almost reverently, like a museum piece. "Thanks, Donald. Now, could you help me with these boxes? They are full of papers and documents, and they are quite heavy.

"Sure, be glad to, right after your going-away reception. The memo in the employee lounge said that everyone at the paper was invited. They're going to pop some champagne."

"Yeah, I can't wait. Speeches and champagne, that's all I need." A perfect ending, some might say.

Standing in the doorway, Donald said, "This place will never be the same. All these certificates and awards, and the photos of you with all the big shots, the governors, and the senators, and that one with the President of the United States!"

"Well, that's my next task, Donald: I must choose what I'll take home. Thanks again. I'll see you downstairs in half an hour."

Anne Marie glances at the photos lining the open walls of her loset. She stands and says, "Thanks, dear canaries, for the *souvenance*, ising the French word for remembrance." Moments later, she steps outside onto the sunny patio of the Washburn Home and is greeted by ngie and Mrs. Wiggins.

"Where have you been all this time?" Angie asks.

"Oh, here and there...mostly there," Anne Marie says.

A warm afternoon sun invites further memories of her many years t the Tribune. She sees a younger version of Donald, the handyman. In he main entryway of the newspaper office, he is building a display abinet, and behind the glass front, he places one of the 1940 model Royal ypewriters that the newsroom staff worked with until they were replaced vith computers. As much as everyone wanted to enter the new world of omputer technology, the silence of the workspace had been difficult to dapt to. Anne Marie remembers when the workmen dismantled the onveyor belts that carried the day's news written on pieces of paper from he newsroom to the proofreaders down the hall. The area became so quiet hat all anyone could hear was the rumble of the presses in the rear of the uilding.

"Thank God, we still used phones. Their ring was a constant eminder that we were reporting on the real world," she says to Angie. For me, the noisy newsroom had quickly become a protective haven, a

safe place where we could weave the day's realities into somethin
comforting for the readers."

"Not unlike the convent, in my experience," adds Angie.

"Oh, and I remember so well that day when my *Maman* picked m
up after work. She commented on the noise and asked me how I coul
stand it. I asked her if the shoe shop was quiet, and she never mentione
it again." Angie announces that the sun is hurting her eyes and that sh
will move inside. "Time for our late afternoon medications," she states.

"I will be there in a minute," adds Anne Marie. The memories o
those early days at the newspaper invite other remembrances. She recall
having breakfast at Nichol's Tea Room with Laura, the switchboar
operator, who had shared her dealings with Aylrod. Laura talked about
home for unwed mothers operated by a group of nuns in New Hampshir
Her neighbor had her baby there and the little illegitimate boy had bee
sent to a Catholic orphanage and eventually to a seminary and had bee
ordained a priest. Years later, when Anne Marie met Father Laroche, he
favorite priest at *Notre-Dame* Church, she recalled the conversation wit
Laura. For a long time, Anne Marie had wondered if that priest was th
baby sent to the unwed mothers' home in New Hampshire. Often, she ha
come close to asking him...

"Will you join us for supper?" Angie's question pulled Anne Mari
out of her reverie and she walked into the Washburn Nursing Home.

The next day, at exactly 6:15 p.m. Sergeant Oswald Dubois i
greeted by Betsy at the front desk. She immediately calls Mrs. Wiggin
who hurries to welcome the visitor. "Welcome to our humble nursin
home. Miss Dubois, your aunt, is expecting you in the lounge. Pleas
follow me." Mrs. Wiggins and Betsy exchange glances of admiration a
the visitor walks into the facility.

"Miss Dubois, your nephew is here."

"Wow, Mrs. Wiggins, all this time, you have never called me Miss ubois; it has always been Anne Marie. How formal you have come...is it to impress our visitor?"

Turning to the sergeant, Mrs. Wiggins says, "Ok, it's Anne Marie. ou can forget the formalities. And what should we call you, young an?"

Ozzie ignores the question and rushes into the welcoming arms of s aunt. "Auntie, auntie, *ma tante, ma tante*. You look so spiffy. It's been w long since we've seen each other? You haven't aged one bit."

"Spiffy! Wow, I have not been called that in decades, not since my rly days as a newspaper reporter. Spiffy, I like that. I'll accept it, Ozzie. ome here and sit down. Let us get reacquainted."

For the next half hour, they occupy a corner of the lounge and read out their welcoming words for everyone to admire, exchanging a riety of news at a fast rate. Ozzie wants to know what propelled her to ove into an official residence for the elderly. Anne Marie wants to know w the recruiting business is heading. She asks him how his mother is eling. Ozzie replies that she died four days ago. He quickly adds that he d her body cremated and that he told all the military officials that he as taking several days off to take her ashes for burial in Wisconsin, her rth home.

"I didn't go to Wisconsin. Instead, I came here. I went AWOL. As old you on the phone, I plan to go to Canada and buy the old Dubois mestead in Saint Caesar, Quebec."

"You did what?" Anne Marie says, remembering the question of tonishment her mother used years ago when she applied for a job at the wspaper. "You did what? You are AWOL?"

"Yes, ma tante. I just cannot stand this war in Iraq, I refuse to be e instrument that gets our soldiers killed, I refuse to have anything to with the U.S. military. Yes, I am Absent Without Leave and I'm proud say so. Of course, I could be arrested and prosecuted, which is why I'm ing to Canada. And I hope to talk you into coming with me."

A lengthy moment of silence follows. Anne Marie looks around t room and is relieved to find it empty.

"Wouldn't you like to see Canada, to spend some time on the far your father...my pépére...escaped to? And frankly, ma tante, I will ne your French skills. I'm quite rusty in that area."

"Speaking of French skills, you will need to use the correct nar for the town. It is not Saint Caesar but Saint Césaire. Repeat after m Saing Sayzaire."

"See what I mean. Ah, *ma tante*, as precious as always. I fond remember when I visited you years ago. You were so helpful a welcoming each time I came to Maine those summers when I was junior high school. Do you remember that day we went to the beach.. was at a state park on the ocean. There was you, your *Maman*, and tl guy called Rocky. He was your boyfriend. We had so much fun..."

"Oh, let me interrupt you, Ozzie. I remember that. His name thou was not Rocky, it was Roger Laroche. And, he was not my boyfrier Look, thanks for the invitation to join you on your move to Saint Césai Merci beaucoup, but let me sleep on it. I will have a definite answ tomorrow morning."

By the time supper is over, everyone at the Washburn Home aware of Ozzie's invitation. There is wonderment and envy. Many Anne Marie's fellow residents want more details; some actually urge h to accept the invitation. One of the ladies asks if she could someho convince management to transfer Anne Marie's room to her. "Who w remind you to take your pills?" asked Mrs. Wiggins. Angie insists th Anne Marie use her fancy suitcase and she asks Tom to get it for An Marie from storage in the cellar.

The next morning at exactly 7:30 a.m., Ozzie returns to the Washburn Home and asks for Anne Marie. A few minutes later Angie shows up at the reception desk and introduces herself. The fancy suitcase sits by the desk. Angie lifts it only to determine that it's still empty. Hiding a look of sheer panic, she runs to Anne Marie's room and finds it empty. She glances into the closet and finds everything as it was. "I don't knows what to say," she offers to Sergeant Dubois who has followed her. She summons Mrs. Wiggins and the two enter Anne Marie's room, but before they close the door, Mrs. Wiggins asks Sarge to step back to the reception area and wait there.

Angie knows exactly where to go next. "She's at the church," Angie whispers.

"What?" Mrs. Wiggins questioned.

"Listen, I'll get Tom and we'll go get her. Let's be calm. We'll resolve this."

As the Washburn Home van turns the corner in front of *Notre-Dame de la Consolation*, the three of them see that Anne Marie is sitting on the Memoriam bench with the plaque to Father Laroche. A few minutes later, Angie walks up to her with a questioning look.

"I am too old for adventures," says Anne Marie.

"This is where I am writing my final draft."

Made in United States
North Haven, CT
31 May 2024